MICHAEL LONGLEY was born in Belfast in 1939 and educated at the Royal Belfast Academical Institution and Trinity College Dublin, where he read Classics. He has won many awards, among them the T.S. Eliot Prize, the Queen's Gold Medal, the PEN Pinter Prize and the inaugural Yakamochi Medal. He was appointed CBE in 2010, and from 2007 to 2010 was Ireland Professor of Poetry. He has published thirteen collections, the most recent being *The Slain Birds*. In 2022 he was awarded the prestigious Feltrinelli International Poetry Prize for a lifetime's achievement. He is a Freeman of the City of Belfast where he and his wife, the critic Edna Longley, live and work.

FRANK ORMSBY was born in Enniskillen, County Fermanagh, in 1947 and was educated at Queen's University Belfast. Until 2010 he was Head of English at the Royal Belfast Academical Institution. He was editor of *The Honest Ulsterman* from 1969 to 1989 and has also edited a number of books and anthologies, including *The Collected Poems of John Hewitt* and *A Rage for Order: Poetry of the Northern Ireland Troubles*. *Goat's Milk: New & Selected Poems* includes work from his four previous collections: *A Store of Candles*, *A Northern Spring*, *The Ghost Train* and *Fireflies*, together with new poems. It was shortlisted for the Christopher Ewart-Biggs Memorial Prize. His latest collections are *The Darkness of Snow* and *The Rain Barrel*. From 2019 to 2022, he was Ireland Professor of Poetry. He lives in Belfast.

JOHN HEWITT

Selected Poems

edited by
MICHAEL LONGLEY
& FRANK ORMSBY

First published in 2007 by Blackstaff Press
an imprint of Colourpoint Creative Ltd
Colourpoint House
Jubilee Business Park
21 Jubilee Road
Newtownards BT23 4YH

Reprinted 2022

With the assistance of the Arts Council of Northern Ireland

LOTTERY FUNDED

© Poems, the Estate of John Hewitt, 1928–86
© Selection and Introduction,
Michael Longley and Frank Ormsby, 2007
All rights reserved

The editors have asserted their right under the Copyright,
Designs and Patents Act 1988 to be identified as the authors of this work.

Printed and bound by Clays Ltd, Elcograf S.p.A.

A CIP catalogue for this book is available from the British Library

ISBN 978-0-85640-802-1

www.blackstaffpress.com

I am the green shoot asking for the flower

JOHN HEWITT
'The Green Shoot'

CONTENTS

INTRODUCTION	xi
EDITORS' NOTE	xxvii
from Conacre	1
Once Alien Here	8
First Corncrake	9
East Antrim Winter	10
The Swathe Uncut	11
Lyric ('Let but a thrush begin …')	12
Lyric ('Chestnut and beech …')	13
Leaf	14
Load	15
Frost	16
Ghosts	17
Mykonos	19
Mycenae and Epidaurus	20
Turf-Carrier on Aranmore	21
Because I Paced My Thought	23
The Green Shoot	24
First Snow in the Glens	26
Colour	27
Landscape	28
The Ram's Horn	29
O Country People	30
Man Fish and Bird	32
The Colony	36

The Stoat	41
The Watchers	42
Hedgehog	43
Rite, Lubitavish, Glenaan	44
The Owl	45
The Municipal Gallery Revisited, October 1954	47
Ossian's Grave, Lubitavish, County Antrim	49
The Frontier	51
Jacob and the Angel	52
An Irishman in Coventry	53
Whit Monday	55
My Grandmother's Garter	56
April Awake	58
Footing Turf	59
Sunset over Glenaan	60
May Altar	62
The Ballad	63
The Wake	64
The Bell	65
The Hill-Farm	66
Gloss, on the Difficulties of Translation	67
An Ulsterman	68
The Dilemma	69
Street Names	70
The Coasters	71
Black and White	74
The Storm	75
From the Chinese of Wang Li Shi	76
Chinese Fluteplayer	77
Emily Dickinson	78
Scissors for a One-Armed Tailor	79
Grey and White	80
Skypiece	81

I Write For …	82
The Search	83
From the Tibetan	85
Et Tu in Arcadia Vixisti	87
The Scar	88
Mary Hagan, Islandmagee, 1919	89
The King's Horses	90
Cultra Manor: The Ulster Folk Museum	91
Neither an Elegy nor a Manifesto	92
A Birthday Rhyme for Roberta	95
Substance and Shadow	96
Encounter Nineteen Twenty	97
A Mobile Mollusc	98
A Local Poet	99
For a Moment of Darkness Over the Nations	100
The Romantic	101
The Glens of Antrim	102
The Blossomed Thorn	103
A Father's Death	104
from Sonnets for Roberta (1954)	105
A Happy Boy	106
Balloons and Wooden Guns	107
The Volunteer	108
The Magician	109
Orchard Country	110
The Doctor's Bag	111
A Holy Place	112
My Sister	113
The Irish Dimension	114
Carnations	115
I Lie Alone	116
The Glens	117
The Man from Malabar	118

The Covenanter's Grave	119
A House Demolished	120
The Christmas Rhymers, Ballynure, 1941	121
For Roberta in the Garden	122
The Hedgehog: For R.	123
To the People of Dresden	124
from Freehold	125
Ulster Names	135
INDEX OF TITLES	139

INTRODUCTION

I

At several points in his life John Hewitt defined his formative influences and essential hierarchies. In the foreword to his *Collected Poems 1932–1967*, for example, he describes himself as 'by birth, an Irishman of Planter stock, by profession an art gallery man, politically a man of the Left' and insists on the relevance of all these factors to the 'conditioning of [his] response to experience'. This statement is prompted by his concern that the poems by which he has been most frequently represented in anthologies might lead readers to think of him as exclusively a nature poet: it remains a useful reminder of his thematic range and most fruitful obsessions.

John Harold Hewitt was born at 96 Cliftonpark Avenue, Belfast, on 28 October 1907. He had his earliest education at Agnes Street National School, the Methodist elementary school where his father was principal. He was of 'Planter stock' on his father's side, the Hewitts having left 'the ripe England of the mounded downs', probably in the seventeenth century, to settle in the Kilmore area of County Armagh. The 'man of the Left' had his origins in Hewitt's Methodist background and in the passionate and practical socialism of his father, to whose liberal values he frequently pays tribute. It was on his father's bookshelves that he discovered, for example, the English radical tradition that included the

Diggers, the Levellers and the Chartists. While still a boy he had begun to accompany his father to political meetings. His earliest poems appeared (*c.* 1928) in left-wing newspapers and periodicals. Hewitt was also inspired by the socialist writings of William Morris, by his many-sidedness and range of concerns. While a student at Queen's University Belfast he borrowed ten shillings from his mother to buy a five-volume second-hand set of Morris's *The Earthly Paradise*. The literary-romantic strain that he found there further excited Hewitt into poetry and led him to the work of W.B. Yeats. He described Morris as 'my first, life-long love among the poets'.

Hewitt's love of art and his career as an 'art gallery man' also had their origins among his father's books and were nurtured later by Morris's writings on art (particularly after Hewitt was employed as an art assistant at the Belfast Museum and Art Gallery in 1930). He helped to form a progressive art group called the Ulster Unit, which included John Luke and Colin Middleton. Throughout the thirties he immersed himself in Irish culture and history, particularly that of his own province. His gallery work involved looking after 'portraits and relics of notable men of Planter stock' (such as the American presidents of Ulster descent), as well as images of radical Presbyterians of the late eighteenth century, such as James Hope and Mary Ann McCracken. He has recorded how these encounters significantly extended what he called his 'local imaginative mythology'. One result was 'The Bloody Brae: A Dramatic Poem' (finished in 1936), Hewitt's first considerable attempt to grapple with the troubled relationship between English and Scottish planters and native Irish in the north of Ireland. At this time he met Roberta Black, whom he married in 1934. They worked together as members of the Belfast Peace League and the British Civil Liberties Union, as well as attending summer schools run by the Independent Labour Party in England.

Hewitt was further energised in the late thirties and early forties by his growing interest in the concept of regionalism, as propounded by Lewis Mumford and other theorists of community. After the outbreak of World War II travel abroad was heavily restricted and Hewitt's regionalist fervour was in part, as he himself admitted, 'a reaction to the isolationism of the war years'. He worked as an unpaid lecturer for the Department of Extra-Mural Studies at Queen's University, and travelled to army camps in Antrim, Down and Armagh to lecture on art and Marxism (after the USSR entered the war on the side of the Allies). The Hewitts began their love affair with the Glens of Antrim at this time. His deepening sense of his own place made Hewitt even more receptive to the regionalist concept of dynamic allegiance to a grouping 'smaller than the nation, larger than the family', which would galvanise artistic life and, in the north of Ireland, potentially transcend sectarian division.

In 1950 Hewitt was promoted to deputy director and keeper of art at the Belfast Museum and Art Gallery, but when the directorship became vacant he was denied the post, having been branded, as he put it, 'communist and pro-Catholic'. The outcome was that he left Belfast for Coventry in 1957 to become art director of the new Herbert Art Gallery. Despite the initial bitter disappointment he later described this move as 'one of the best things that ever happened to me'. Coventry, under the control of an enlightened Labour council, was in the process of being rebuilt after the air raids of 1940 and 1941. It was cosmopolitan and racially mixed, in contrast to the 'ingrown parochialism' of Ireland. 'Image of the state hope argued for', Coventry inspired some of Hewitt's noblest lines:

> I should have made it plain that I stake my future
> on birds flying in and out of the schoolroom window,
> on the council of sunburnt comrades in the sun,
> and the picture carried with singing into the temple.

The 'art gallery man', at the age of fifty, found himself challenged to develop a gallery which as yet possessed no collection. He grew to love the English landscape, and his gallery work allowed him to travel extensively in Europe. Furthermore, the man of Planter stock discovered that the Hewitt family had figured prominently in the history of Coventry, so that his exile was, to an extent, lightened by a sense of homecoming. The tensions of this period generated at least two of Hewitt's finest poems, 'An Irishman in Coventry' and 'The Search'. In 1968 almost four decades of his poetry, which had hitherto appeared mainly in pamphlet form, in magazines and in just the one book-length collection (*No Rebel Word* from 1948), were brought together and given fresh focus in *Collected Poems 1932–1967*.

Civil conflict erupted in Northern Ireland in 1969. Hewitt's exploration of cultural diversity and the legacy of colonialism took on an urgent contemporary dimension. His retirement in 1972 and return to Belfast coincided with the early years of the Troubles. His wife Roberta died in 1975. Despite these sorrows the remaining years of Hewitt's life were richly productive in poetry and prose and brought him considerable recognition and acclaim. He received honorary degrees from the University of Ulster and Queen's University, and was awarded the Gregory Medal by the Irish Academy of Letters. From 1976 to 1979 he was the first writer in residence at Queen's. The Arts Council of Northern Ireland commissioned a film about his life and work, *I Found Myself Alone*. He was elected first President of the Northern Ireland Fabian Society, and in 1983 was made a Freeman of the City of Belfast. His pioneering survey *Art in Ulster I* was followed by monographs on his friends, the painters John Luke and Colin Middleton. In his seminal anthology *Rhyming Weavers and Other Country Poets of Antrim and Down* he retrieved the work of the vernacular 'bards' who wrote in Scots and were significant muses for him:

> He followed their lilting stanzas
> through a thousand columns or more,
> and scratched for the splintered couplets
> in the cracks on the cottage floor,
> for his Rhyming Weavers fell silent
> when they flocked through the factory door.

He revised and recast material from his manuscript note- books, and published new collections including *Out of My Time*, *Time Enough*, *The Rain Dance*, *Mosaic* and his sequence of autobiographical sonnets *Kites in Spring: A Belfast Boyhood*.

John Hewitt died at his home in Stockmans Lane in June 1987. Later that year *Ancestral Voices: The Selected Prose of John Hewitt* (edited by Tom Clyde) was published. *Collected Poems* followed in 1991. The first John Hewitt International Summer School was held in 1988 at Garron Tower in the Glens of Antrim. Hewitt bequeathed his body to medical research and asked that there be no funeral service. A week after his death more than three hundred people gathered, by word of mouth, in the Lyric Theatre – poets, writers, broadcasters, scholars, shipyard workers, trade unionists, lawyers, politicians, clergymen, priests, actors, painters. We read his poems and exchanged memories and stories. We were celebrating a local hero and an exceptional poet.

II

John Hewitt begins one of his most celebrated poems 'The Ram's Horn' with a resonant line: 'I have turned to the landscape because men disappoint me.' A good deal of his finest poetry is set in the Ulster countryside, especially the Glens of Antrim where he and his wife Roberta rented a holiday cottage at Tiveragh:

> And though to keep my brain and body alive
> I need the honey of the city hive,
> I also need for nurture of the heart
> the rowan berries and the painted cart,
> the bell at noon, the scythesman in the corn,
> the cross of rushes, and the fairy thorn.

His city-man's urge to understand the structures of rural life, his affectionate, enquiring descriptions of seasonal tasks, his celebrations of weather and landscape extend the pastoral tradition of Edward Thomas, Thomas Hardy and John Clare. And there are more distant echoes, from Old Irish Poetry ('The Blackbird of Belfast Lough' from the ninth century) and Virgil's *Georgics*. It is tempting at first to think of him as being mainly a nature poet, a sort of Northern Irish neo-Georgian. But he is altogether a more complex figure than these terms suggest. From the very beginning he is an elegiac celebrant – 'one whose gaze is on the end of things', one for whom 'a tree is truer for its being bare'. Even his delightful animal poems are psychologically unsettled. Although one of the pleasures of reading this poet is sharing his surprise when he encounters 'the crouching hedgehog' and 'the frightened hare', and all those birds (corncrake, 'crook-necked heron', 'speckled gannets'), animals represent for him 'the world of things I know and do not know'. The 'grey badger' makes him feel that 'It was as if another nature came / close to my knowledge, but could not be known'. In 'The Stoat' nature's shattering violence finds its 'codicil' in a broken shell: 'a little yoke, a golden sixpence, lay, / a fallen sun in a wrecked universe'. He is often in the silent company of his wife as they stalk and scrutinise creatures – 'the wren's intentions in a bare thorn hedge', or the owl 'that watched you watch with steady eyes'. These lyrics read like oblique love poems about awakenings and self-definition: 'for one instant out of time, / we had been seen and recognised'. When Hewitt writes in the closing stanza of 'The Ram's Horn' that 'I live my best in the landscape, being at ease there', he is speaking relatively.

In Hewitt's pastoral poems the disquiet is social as well as psychological. As a city man drawn to the countryside, he finds that he is both fulfilled and excluded there, that the poet is defined by the landscape while to the people who live in it he is an outsider. 'O country people, you of the hill farms': his address is full of yearning, but he knows that 'there is a wide bog between us, a high wall' and that 'I could not change enough, and you will not change'. He realises sadly that in the eyes of the countrymen he loves no achievement of his will ever have the importance of

> even a phrase or a story which will come
> pat to the tongue, part of the tapestry
> of apt response, at the appropriate time,
> like a wise saw, a joke, an ancient rime
> used when the last stack's topped at the day's end,
> or when the last lint's carted round the bend.

Despite this loss Hewitt, typically, knows his own worth and asserts it:

> No tweed-bright poet drunk in pastoral
> or morris-dances in the legion hall,
> I know my farmer and my farmer's wife,
> the squalid focus of their huxter life,
> the grime-veined fists, the thick rheumatic legs,
> the cracked voice gloating on the price of eggs …

'And yet this is too savage', he says, and he recalls

> the friendly doors and hearths of Donegal,
> the red heels in the ash, the turf blown ripe
> tonged up and held to light the broken pipe …

A discreet drama is enacted throughout his poetry as he argues with himself, tests his stance and position. He contradicts himself because he is trying always to understand. Diffidence follows certainty, withdrawal follows assertion. His most generous embraces carry with them a hint of *noli me tangere*.

The city man's feelings of exclusion in the countryside modulate painfully into the Planter's apprehensive desire to be assimilated into Catholic Ireland and yet remain true to himself. He calls Ireland 'this ruptured country'. He despairs of 'my creed-haunted, godforsaken race'. He sorrows for 'the children that today / rage in the fetters of their fathers' fears'. Coming from a Methodist background he fears the Catholics' 'creed as we have always feared / the lifted hand against unfettered thought'. And yet it is this sense of difference that inspires one of the most tender moments in all his work. In 'The Hill-Farm' he finds himself outside a neighbour's home in the Glens of Antrim as the rosary is being said (a scene which sparked off its mirror-opposite in Seamus Heaney's equally civilised 'The Other Side'):

> At each Hail Mary, Full of Grace,
> I pictured every friendly face,
> clenched in devotion of a kind
> alien to my breed and mind,
> easy as breathing, natural
> as birds that fly, as leaves that fall;
> yet with a sense that I still stood
> far from that faith-based certitude,
> here in the vast enclosing night,
> outside its little ring of light.

These religious and political tensions inspire some of Hewitt's most radical thinking, in prose as well as poetry, and animate his philosophy of regionalism. This celebrated passage from his essay 'Regionalism: The Last Chance' sounds as relevant today as it did in 1947:

> Ulster, considered as a region and not as a symbol of any particular creed, can, I believe, command the loyalty of every one of its inhabitants. For regional identity does not preclude, rather it requires, membership of a larger association. And, whether that association be, as I hope, of a federated British

> Isles, or a federal Ireland, out of that loyalty to our own place, rooted in honest history, in familiar folkways and knowledge, phrased in our own dialect, there should emerge a culture and an attitude individual and distinctive, a fine contribution to the European inheritance and no mere echo of the thought and imagination of another people or another land.

In more personal terms he discusses the value of having multiple cultural allegiances, an idea that was hardly fashionable in 1953 when this passage from 'Planter's Gothic' was first published:

> The whole point of the ideal Ulsterman is simply that he must carry within himself elements of both Scots and English with a strong charge of the basic Irish. When I discovered, not long ago, that the old Planter's Gothic tower of Kilmore Church still encloses the stump of a round tower and that it was built on the site of a Culdee holy place, I felt a step nearer to that synthesis. It is the best symbol I have yet found for the strange textures of my response to this island of which I am a native. I may appear Planter's Gothic but there is a round tower somewhere inside, and needled through every sentence I utter.

It is often erroneously assumed that the Ulster Protestant suffers from an identity crisis. Hewitt always remains pretty clear as to who he is (or who he is not). In a 1974 symposium in the *Irish Times* ('The Clash of Identities' edited by Eavan Boland) he sets out what he calls 'my hierarchy of values':

> I'm an Ulsterman, of planter stock. I was born in the island of Ireland, so secondarily I'm an Irishman. I was born in the

British archipelago and English is my native tongue, so I'm British. The British archipelago consists of offshore islands to the continent of Europe, so I'm European.

'Mine is historic Ulster, battlefield / of Gael and Planter.' Several strong poems have a manifesto-like ring to them: 'Once alien here my fathers built their house, / claimed, drained, and gave the land the shapes of use'. Again and again he insists on his Ulster heritage: 'because of all the buried men / in Ulster clay' he feels 'as native in my thought as any here'. Reviewing *Collected Poems* in *Threshold*, Seamus Heaney writes that Hewitt's 'lifelong concern to question and document the relationship between art and locality has provided all subsequent Northern writers with a hinterland of reference.' The poems born out of what Heaney calls 'those accurate, painful quests towards self-knowledge' courageously examine the fears and prejudices of the Planter stock. In 'The Colony', written prophetically in the early fifties, Ulster is thinly disguised as a Roman province:

> Some of us think our leases have run out
> but dig square heels in, keep the roads repaired;
> and one or two loud voices would restore
> the rack, the yellow patch, the curfewed ghetto.

Only after self-questioning can claims be staked. The poem ends with qualified optimism. The Roman mask dissolves, and Hewitt's love for his native province shines through:

> for we have rights drawn from the soil and sky;
> the use, the pace, the patient years of labour,

>   the rain against the lips, the changing light,
>   the heavy clay-sucked stride, have altered us;
>   we would be strangers in the Capitol;
>   this is our country also, nowhere else;
>   and we shall not be outcast on the world.

In his essay 'The Dissidence of Dissent' John Wilson Foster suggests that these lines 'perfectly capture the planter's brittle certainty with its soft centre of despair'. Hewitt may sympathise with the fears of 'my fathers', but he is scathing about the prejudices that were later to debase Unionism and contribute to thirty years of fratricidal violence. In 'From the Tibetan' Unionist placemen are thinly disguised as corrupt lamas. In 'The Coasters' their philistinism and complacent ignorance make the Protestant middle classes complicit in the contagion: 'The cloud of infection hangs over the city, / a quick change of wind and it / might spill over the leafy suburbs'. The refrain is: 'You coasted too long'. Ulster's sectarian barbarities hurt Hewitt into powerful public pronouncement. It was more than a literary event when his lamentation for victims of the Troubles, 'Neither an Elegy nor a Manifesto', was printed in the news pages of the *Irish Times*: 'Bear in mind these dead: / I can find no plainer words'.

As his 'hierarchy of values' indicates, it would be wrong to confine Hewitt to 'historic Ulster, battlefield / of Gael and Planter', even though it is his 'chosen ground'. Crucial though the 'crazy knot' of Irish history is to his thought, his fundamental interest is 'the relation of man to his environment, the shaping and controlling of consciousness by locale, climate and topography', as Terence Brown points out in his pioneering 1975 survey *Northern Voices*. In 'Landscape' Hewitt puts it very precisely: 'So talk of weather is also talk of life, / and life is man and place and these have names'. A laureate of habitation, he appreciates how provisional dwelling and home are. In 'No Rootless Colonist' he writes: 'I have experienced a deep enduring sense of our human past before the Lion Gate at Mycenae and among the Rolright Stones of the Oxfordshire border …' The penultimate stanza of 'Mykonos' is a brilliant tiny chronicle of the human interim:

> Mykonos is a suburb of the hot moon,
> the threshing floors on the slopes, shallow craters.
> Man has not been here long
> and may leave tomorrow.

'The Search' begins as a poem about leaving Belfast to settle in the English Midlands and 'remembering that you are a guest in the house'. It explores what feeling at home might mean, in England or Ireland, and concludes that nowhere can really be 'your abiding place'. The last two lines are quintessential Hewitt: 'what you seek may be no more than / a broken circle of stones on a rough hillside, somewhere'.

This profoundly egalitarian poet is concerned to interact with his readers. He knows that poetry is a communal as well as an individual activity. He avoids verbal pyrotechnics, ostentatious virtuosity. He prefers a plain utterance, a verbal fabric we might call homespun, an address that sounds confidential:

> I write for my own kind,
> I do not pitch my voice
> that every phrase be heard
> by those who have no choice:

> their quality of mind
> must be withdrawn and still,
> as moth that answers moth
> across a roaring hill.

Sympathetic critics can sometimes overemphasise Hewitt's qualities of worthiness, orderliness, decency, decorum. He himself matter-of-factly compares his verse technique to carpentry ('I wrought / along the grain as with a steady tool.'). John Wilson Foster says of Hewitt's prosody: 'Visually his lines are tidy furrows across neat fields or poems; aurally his iambic meters have the regularity of expert but easy ploughing …' Though true of much of the poetry, this assessment does not take into account the syncopated zigzags of Hewitt's free verse ('Man Fish and Bird', 'Gloss, On the Difficulties of Translation'); or the melodic consummation of several brief lyrics ('April Awake', 'The Bell', 'Black and White', 'Colour', 'Skypiece'); or the standing-stone-like grandeur of 'Landscape' and 'Substance and Shadow'; or the denunciatory outbursts of the political satires; or the transcendental intensity of 'The Blossomed Thorn':

> As gazing at it long I stood,
> a strange awareness stirred within,
> not of my flesh becoming wood
> and stinging where the buds begin,
>
> but of a flowing universe
> that poured and streamed towards the tree,
> swept with a magnet's silent force
> into the One Reality.

Lines like these must startle readers who know Hewitt only through the usual anthology pieces. In 'No Rootless Colonist' he claims: 'My cast of mind is such that I am moved by intuitions, intimations, imaginative realisations, epiphanies ...'

John Hewitt is the sort of poet who needs to write a great deal in order to understand himself. He happily contradicts himself. Though it is ultimately indispensable, the sheer bulk of the *Collected Poems* of 1991 can be dispiriting. There's a danger of thick foliage obscuring the loveliest flowers. It has been exhilarating to clear space for the ninety-five poems (plus extracts from his two extended meditations, 'Conacre' and 'Freehold') that in our judgement showcase Hewitt's accomplishments and variety. Although poems we have loved for many years provide the backbone of this selection, it has been a particular excitement to rediscover work that comes at us as from out of the blue. Hewitt the prophetic predecessor of the so-called Ulster Renaissance is now widely acclaimed, 'the daddy of us all' as James Simmons called him. More intimately appreciated is the poet whose return to Belfast in 1972 bestowed winter sunshine on our damaged community. Whilst editing this *Selected Poems* we have come to revere another John Hewitt. He is as unforeseeable as 'The Man from Malabar' who 'lifts a wavering song, / meandering along':

> And somewhere on the rim
> of that strange haunting cry
> a cadence makes its way,
> an old song wanders home,
> to summon to the thought
> a country crossroads fair –
> a strain some singer caught
> out of the misty air.

MICHAEL LONGLEY & FRANK ORMSBY
NOVEMBER 2006

EDITORS' NOTE

The poems in this selection are ordered chronologically in accordance with their publication in book form, as was the case in *The Collected Poems of John Hewitt* (edited by Frank Ormsby, 1991). Where a poem is reprinted without alteration in more than one collection, we have placed it in its original context. Where Hewitt has revised a poem from an earlier collection for inclusion in a later, we have included the later version only, in its appropriate place.

from CONACRE

'Conacre: an Irish land system; the letting by a tenant
for a season, of small portions of land ready ploughed
and prepared for a crop'

OED

For memory's sake indulgent I repeat
the marvel of that dawn when you and I
rose when the stars commanded all the sky,
and on the dry road under the windless firs
heard the first bird that stirs before light stirs,
and took the steep lane to the brackened crest,
and stood to see the water's dark unrest,
wet to the knees with dew and shivering,
and watched a black shag cross with hurried wing
close to the surface of the roaring bay.
We waited for the sun. To the east there lay
a cloud that hid its rising. Quickly one by one
the stars were snuffed. We waited for the sun.
Above cold Garron's cape in lucid air
one star remained. The sky was high and bare,
save for that cloudbank, growing golden now,
and little scattered gusts in bush and bough
troubled the dry leaves, rasped the thistle crown
ripe with the autumn. Where the wrack was brown
small sea fowl started on their sleek routine.
The peak of Lurigedan now was green
in brighter light, but still the sun delayed.

We turned disheartened. Suddenly you said
and pointed, 'Look.' Behind above the trees
a crook-necked heron flapped with patient ease
and passing over, flew ahead as if
slow missile aimed at Scotland. Down the cliff
chagrined we took our way. The hour was gone
that should have marked the coming of the dawn.

We reached the dewcrisp sand and turned again;
the wakened world still lacked the noise of men,
though in the nearest house blue smoke began
to mingle with the leaves. A rabbit ran
over the salt short grass. The grazing sheep
came stumbling from the hedges lame with sleep
to browse along the rough. And then at once
we strode to where the river cuts the stones
after a lazy drift, bog-brown and slow
between steep banks where grey-leaved salleys grow,
and saw a speckled gannet poise on wing
to fall like hurtling pebble from a sling,
deadly as David, clean and pitiless
as later sparrowhawk for wren's distress
we ran to check from havoc in the hedge
half-hid by nettles at the first tee's edge.
Then turning for a last look at the sea,
we gasped amazed. The thing we came to see
had happened when our foolish backs were turned.
The cloud had lifted and below it burned,
hot brass upon the water, a bar of sun
like moon fantastic, and the job was done.
Our little world was younger by a day,
and we paced proudly home the longer way,
aware of every freshly spiring scent
as benediction and as sacrament.

. . . .

You would escape from brick but not too far.
You want the hill at hand familiar,
the punctual packet and the telephone,
that you may not be lonely when alone.

I nod assent, no dusty pioneer
complaining that the road has come too near,
but one who needs the comfortable pace
of safe tradition. Reckon from my face
and its smooth lazy cheeks, the close-set eyes,
the tight-shut mouth aggressive that belies
the hand that scarce dare push a latchless gate,
and you will gauge me hero in debate
who funks decisions nor will shift his hams
save to applause for savage epigrams
which skim a laugh and leave mistrust behind
that one so harsh insists he still is kind –
I warp and wrench the canvas that was meant
for nothing more than gentle sentiment
with this coarse introspection. I began
these verses to discover why a man,
townbred and timid, should attain to peace
with outworn themes and rustic images,
and now I find the shifting meaning turns
on human history and its wry concerns.
I should have guessed what other men have known,
that definition means comparison,
and that we find our lightest words demand
a cosmos weighed within a human hand,
and that our logic must be stretched to include
the coral insect, cancer in the blood,

the crazy atom, and the crocodile,
the twitching nerve that's knotted to a smile,
and that the simple shock at spilling salt
implies the murdered prophet in the vault,
the grave da Vinci's mural and the plans
that left hand drew to father bombing planes.
For every act is like that ivory sphere
some turbaned rascal carved in high Kashmir
that holds another and another yet,
till eye blurs groping for the infinite.
The surfaces of life are safer stuff;
if weather tear the husk it is enough.
Should we persist and split the final pod,
who knows if it reveal the seed of God?

. . . .

This is my home and country. Later on
perhaps I'll find this nation is my own;
but here and now it is enough to love
this faulted ledge, this map of cloud above,
and the great sea that beats against the west
to swamp the sun.

                No single season's best.
I think in autumn, when the seed's afield,
the year is crowned. But black in winter, stilled
by a clean frost, the trees are lovelier;
and then in spring, with song and sap astir,
I touch a peak of joy that lasts until
the hawthorn in the quarry-gutted hill
brims the warm air, or from a cairn-tipped mound
the whole loughside is an enchanted ground

with crowded fruit, and dazzled waters spread
layer after layer of gold, and overhead
the weary rooks are burnished as they come
through yellow light laboriously home.

Once in a summer, stepping slow again
through the lush homage of a shadowed lane
with one released from privacy of pain
remarking with now unimprisoned eyes
the shepherd's purse, the barren strawberries,
just where the ruts run in past pillared stone
the mossy foot-track to the stream goes down,
there on a tall beech close against the sky
an evening thrush was calling stridently,
lost in the leaves at first, discovered on
the utmost branch, his breast toward the sun;
no nestlings' clamour and no rivals' threat
to vex his peace with danger or with debt,
he simply sang and sang for naked zest,
shouting the mellow sun down the submissive west.

We stood to marvel, silent at his skill;
the cruising bee in clover too was still.
So, thought I in that instant, should my art
make joy its theme, were but the troubled heart
released from anger, severed from dismay
for the last hour of my declining day.

. . . .

No tweed-bright poet drunk in pastoral
or morris-dances in the legion hall
I know my farmer and my farmer's wife,
the squalid focus of their huxter life,

the grime-veined fists, the thick rheumatic legs,
the cracked voice gloating on the price of eggs,
the miser's Bible, and the tedious aim
to add another boggy acre to the name.

And yet this is too savage.
                              I recall
the friendly doors and hearths of Donegal,
the red heels in the ash, the turf blown ripe
tonged up and held to light the broken pipe,
and the stooped father mingling puff with puff,
talking of labour when the world was rough
in lowland barns or where the track was thrust
across the range or through the prairie dust;
and I remember one who sat and swayed
in island kitchen till we were afraid
of ghost or grugach for she filled the glen
with shadowy forms of fierce fanatic men
and left us for the midnight's rainy squall
to hobble past them with a tugging shawl;
or that deaf man who stopped us on a bridge
across the lough-end where no tree or hedge
covers the tilted slabs of rain-grained stone,
and in slow phrases bellowed one by one
offered a chance of poaching if I'd care,
then, pressing more, if I'd the heart to dare.

Now after twenty years I recollect
old Brennan scrawny, long and freckle-necked,
padding the floor with thick and matted sock
and stretching to adjust the German clock,
and as he winds, gazing with tireless eyes
on the framed picture of his famous prize –

a bull, a cup, a man beside the bull –
the day he won, the cup was splashing full:
and that slow man who loves the faery thorn,
and never fails to fork new cribs of corn
for his few heifers when the old year ends,
who calls the hare and badger both his friends,
yet turns no back on progress, dreaming still
of the broad tractors sweeping up the hill,
and the great binder worked by equal men,
lifting its swathes of fat collective grain.
So in this hope which harbours all I love
as rain-chill fist slips grateful into glove,
as the soft plastic gathers from the mould
a strength by its loose atoms unforetold,
I rest content. No contradictions vex
the single mind unfriended, or perplex
the will that finds no longer life to waste
so clear the path imperative is traced;
the heart's conscripted with its plunging blood;
the place is past for wilful attitude;
so ends my passion, ends my lonely rage,
hushed in perspectives of the Golden Age.

ONCE ALIEN HERE

Once alien here my fathers built their house,
claimed, drained, and gave the land the shapes of use,
and for their urgent labour grudged no more
than shuffled pennies from the hoarded store
of well-rubbed words that had left their overtones
in the ripe England of the mounded downs.
The sullen Irish limping to the hills
bore with them the enchantments and the spells
that in the clans' free days hung gay and rich
on every twig of every thorny hedge,
and gave the rain-pocked stone a meaning past
the blurred engraving of the fibrous frost.

So I, because of all the buried men
in Ulster clay, because of rock and glen
and mist and cloud and quality of air
as native in my thought as any here,
who now would seek a native mode to tell
our stubborn wisdom individual,
yet lacking skill in either scale of song,
the graver English, lyric Irish tongue,
must let this rich earth so enhance the blood
with steady pulse where now is plunging mood
till thought and image may, identified,
find easy voice to utter each aright.

FIRST CORNCRAKE

We heard the corncrake's call from close at hand,
and took the lane that led us near the noise;
a hedged half-acre, flanked by sycamore,
was his small wedge of world. We crouched and peered
through the close thorn. The moving cry again
swivelled our gaze. Time whispered in the leaves.
A tall ditch-grass blade rocked as a languid bee
brushed the dry sliver with a rasping wing.

In silence still we watched; a careless heel
smashing a twig husk, grating on the grit,
and winning for itself a warning glance.
Then, when strung patience seemed about to yawn
as if the world demanded leave to move
on its slung reeling pitch about the sun,
I saw a head, a narrow pointed head
stirring among the brown weed-mottled grass
as the monotonous and edgy voice
kept up its hard complaint. I held the spot
in a fixed gaze. The brown head disappeared,
was seen in seconds in another clump,
and for a blessed moment, full in sight
the brown bird, brighter than the book foresaw,
stood calling in a little pool of grass.
I moved a finger and you shared the joy
that chance till then had never offered us.

It would have been a little grief to know
this punctual cry each year, and yet grow old
without one glimpse of him that made the cry.
The heart still hankers for the rounded shape.

EAST ANTRIM WINTER

Wet roads between black hedges, and a sky
faint yellow-green with sunset, ribbed by trees
all stripped to twigs. Unregimented, loose,
rooks flap for home with slow and easy beat
from the dark furrows that this morning's plough
ripped over the bleached stubble. At the bridge
the glutted ripples crowd beneath the arch,
each spined with light like twinkling stickleback,
or idly turn aside and coast the stones
that held the withered lichen since the floods
of August draped each nape with wisps of straw.
White in the distance in the dayli'gone
move fists and faces, metal to the light
the cycle's wheel-rims and a swinging can.
Only a lonely blackbird cries aloud,
near hand but out of sight.

                                      Sun's tide recedes,
then darkens as a cap of cloud descends;
but no lamp wakens in the scattered farms.
The moon will rise on a defeated world.

THE SWATHE UNCUT

As the brown mowers strode across the field
shapes fled before them thrusting back the grain,
till in a shrinking angle unrevealed
the frightened hare crouched back, the last at bay,
for even the corncrake, blind in his dismay,
had found the narrow safety of the drain.

And so of old the country folk declared
the last swathe holds a wayward fugitive,
uncaught, moth-gentle, tremulously scared,
that must be, by the nature of all grain,
the spirit of the corn that should be slain
if the saved seed will have the strength to live.

Then by their ancient ritual they sought
to kill the queen, the goddess, and ensure
that her spent husk and shell be safely brought
to some known corner of beneficence,
lest her desired and lively influence
be left to mock the next plough's signature.

So I have figured in my crazy wit
in this flat island sundered to the west
the last swathe left uncut, the blessed wheat
wherein still free the gentle creatures go
instinctively erratic, rash or slow,
unregimented, never yet possessed.

LYRIC

Let but a thrush begin
or colour catch my eye,
maybe a spring-woke whin
under a reeling sky,

and all at once I lose
mortality's despair,
having so much to choose
out of the teeming air.

LYRIC

Chestnut and beech
sycamore and willow
with one chill touch
of autumn are yellow.

Even the alder
slanting over the river
is cold and older
than you shall be ever

who hold a thought
with a simple passion
shall last through drought
to the rainy season.

LEAF

O fall of the leaf I am tired,
with this sunset let me be still.
The tips of the stubble are fired
by the slanted blade of the sun
sheathing his flame in the hill.
Let me smoulder so and be done.

The withered leaf tumbles and turns
over lazy islands of air,
more lively now as it burns
than when it was green overhead.
Let me draw from autumnal despair
the strength to be tired without dread.

The pigeons, a dozen and two,
take a half-mile circle of light:
they are washed in the green and the blue
and the delicate gold of the sky.
Let me narrow in on my night
with that effortless certainty.

LOAD

Today we carted home the last brown sheaf
and hooked the scythe against the dry barn wall:
the yellow border's on the chestnut leaf,
the beech leaf's yellow all.

Tomorrow we must bring the apples in,
they are as big as they shall ever be:
already starlings eager to begin
have tasted many a tree.

And in the garden, all the roses done,
the light lies gently, faint and almost cold,
on withered golden-rod and snapdragon
and tarnished marigold.

FROST

With frost again the thought is clear and wise
that rain made dismal with a mist's despair,
the raw bleak earth beneath cloud-narrowed skies
finds new horizons in the naked air.
Light leaps along the lashes of the eyes;
a tree is truer for its being bare.

So must the world seem keen and very bright
to one whose gaze is on the end of things,
who knows, past summer lush, brimmed autumn's height,
no promise in the inevitable springs,
all stripped of shadow down to bone of light,
the false songs gone and gone the restless wings.

GHOSTS

I have no ghosts.
               My dead are safely dead:
my grandfather reading the paper, my grandmother
fumbling in cupboards, my uncle with his clubs
standing idly, his left hand licked by the dog,
or walking rapidly talking of Mark Twain.

These are flat pictures flickering in the mind
with focus narrowing, widening, blurring, lost.
They are not repeating these acts on another plane,
and when they did them they were not shadows of things
but suffering creatures moving with pain or joy.

They survive now only in the brittle thoughts
of a dwindling group of people.
                            If I could
gather the scattered colours and shapes and words
that are left in minds of a dozen friends growing old
any manikin I'd make would never stir.

The winter evening reading and asking questions
while my grandfather straightened his tasselled cap
and gave the answer, had surely spun a cable
that should hold when the hesitant flesh had disappeared.
I knew his mind and mocked him and loved him well;
he knew my rash opinions and jeered at them.

Yet he is dead and has not whispered a word,
or shifted a glass of water on a table.
I even begin to forget the sound of his voice.

Died first to the active senses, dying again
to the senses in memory, touch and hearing are gone;
only a listless eye remembers his face.

MYKONOS

This dun-coloured island, dry and coarse as a cinder,
with no past to speak of, let alone sing,
anchored in the pulsating shadow
of that holy place, Delos.

Humped-up out of the dark water,
with steep granite edges,
not low in the gunwale or nearly awash,
like its neighbour, with history.

Not a single broken column
with the fluted drums disjointed like vertebrae,
nor mutilated torso, boulder-big,
to ballast it.

Delos may fill some with a strange sadness
at the presence of shadowy crowds
in the narrow streets, in the *agora*,
slippering over the ruined mosaics.

Mykonos is a suburb of the hot moon,
the threshing floors on the slopes, shallow craters.
Man has not been here long
and may leave tomorrow.

Even that proud old woman in black,
high on her wide-laden donkey,
brown face shawled, dark eyes bright,
is only passing this way.

MYCENAE AND EPIDAURUS

Across the scorched stubble among the grey olives
the thin black goats and the old woman with the distaff
inhabited a landscape hard and simple,
but impossible to share.

On the broken hillside with the dry-stone
walls and the deep-paddocked grave-pits,
Cuchullain and Oisin leaped suddenly to mind;
and I could have joined in the shouting
as the small clouds of chariot-dust
exploded up the long slope –
could have joined in the loud chant
as the shod-wheels sparked in the rutted stone,
for a poem's span,
too absolute to be endured longer.

But only near the dark green grove
with the pine-scent and the light airs
among the fronded fans,
was I somehow strangely at home,
receiving, open, myself;
tiered far back in that pin-drop theatre
or beside the square pit
with its shock-therapy of snakes.

TURF-CARRIER
ON ARANMORE

The small boy drove the shaggy ass
out of the yard along the track,
rutted between two dry-stone walls,
his errand guessed from half-built stack.
Barefoot he tripped behind its tail,
too shy to lag and stride with us:
an older lad would match our pace
and snatch some topic to discuss.
He swung his switch, a salley rod,
his bleached head glinting in the sun,
but only flicked his ragged thighs
and pattered nonchalantly on.

We spoke no word. The boy, the ass,
the rutted path across the bare
unprofitable mountainside,
were native to this Druid air.
But, as we followed, rag and patch,
the string which braced each splintered creel,
the bald, rubbed flank, the hooves unshod,
growing awry and down-at-heel,
so woke our pity, I pronounced
a bitter sentence to condemn
the land that bred such boys and beasts
to starve the beauty out of them.

The small boy heard, not quite my words,
but, rather say, my angry tone;
a bright blush warmed his sunburnt neck;
he struck a sharp and jolting bone,
and turned the ass with prod and cry
through the first gap that caught his glance,
although the ruts roamed on ahead
to meet the bog's black-trenched expanse,
misjudging my intent and sure
that we were proud and critical.
Your father's beast is very dear,
if you are poor, if you are small.

BECAUSE I PACED
MY THOUGHT

Because I paced my thought by the natural world,
the earth organic, renewed with the palpable seasons,
rather than the city falling ruinous, slowly
by weather and use, swiftly by bomb and argument,

I found myself alone who had hoped for attention.
If one listened a moment he murmured his dissent:
this is an idle game for a cowardly mind.
The day is urgent. The sun is not on the agenda.

And some who hated the city and man's unreasoning acts
remarked: He is no ally. He does not say that
Power and Hate are the engines of human treason.
There is no answering love in the yellowing leaf.

I should have made it plain that I stake my future
on birds flying in and out of the schoolroom window,
on the council of sunburnt comrades in the sun,
and the picture carried with singing into the temple.

THE GREEN SHOOT

In my harsh city, when a Catholic priest,
known by his collar, padded down our street,
I'd trot beside him, pull my schoolcap off
and fling it on the ground and stamp on it.

I'd catch my enemy, that errand boy,
grip his torn jersey and admonish him
first to admit his faith and, when he did,
repeatedly to curse the Pope of Rome;

schooled in such duties by my bolder friends;
yet not so many hurried years before,
when I slipped in from play one Christmas Eve
my mother bathed me at the kitchen fire,

and wrapped me in a blanket for the climb
up the long stairs; and suddenly we heard
the carol singers somewhere in the dark,
their voices sharper, for the frost was hard.

My mother carried me though the dim hall
into the parlour, where the only light
upon the patterned wall and furniture
came from the iron lamp across the street;

and there looped round the lamp the singers stood,
but not on snow in grocers' calendars,
singing a song I liked until I saw
my mother's lashes were all bright with tears.

Out of this mulch of ready sentiment,
gritty with threads of flinty violence,
I am the green shoot asking for the flower,
soft as the feathers of the snow's cold swans.

FIRST SNOW IN THE GLENS

When the winter sky, snow-ominous, crowds in,
here at the wood's edge is the world's end;
the valley cockcrow, the bleat of sheep on the hills
hint of a wider stage, like friendly rumours,
but our immediate place is an island in time.

Chopping the twigs on a stump till the dull blood sang
(my arm beats still with the unaccustomed labour)
I too was a warm oasis-island of joy,
watching the first light flakes, and hearing the leaves,
dry on the hard ground, whisper salutation,
hearing the robin's chirr, and following
the wren's intentions in a bare thorn hedge;
for no large life, this hour, shall intersect
my patient curves; since even the hooded hag
tying her faggot of kindling, garrulous,
and John MacNaghten, that slow friendly lad,
clumping up the lane to his snares in the whins,
and at a distance, striding through slant flakes,
a man, not seen before, with bag and gun,
have the same lease and something of the nature
of rocking branch, of blackbird, bluetit, wren.

COLOUR

Moved to the blessing of colour
because of the marvellous whin
and over the clay-fleshed plowland
the young corn brairded green,
I name each colour for blessing,
for blessing's the grace of delight;
the bud the leaf and the blossom
till I rise to the mercy of white.
I bless the cloud and the seagull,
the blackthorn and hawthorn bless,
the lamb and the farmer's daughter
in her Confirmation dress.

LANDSCAPE

For a countryman the living landscape is
a map of kinship at one level,
at another, just below this, a chart of use,
never at any level a fine view:
sky is a handbook of labour or idleness;
wind in one airt is the lapping of hay,
in another a long day at turf on the moss;
landscape is families, and a lone man
boiling a small pot, and letters once a year;
it is also, underpinning this, good corn
and summer grazing for sheep free of scab
and fallow acres waiting for the lint.
So talk of weather is also talk of life,
and life is man and place and these have names.

THE RAM'S HORN

I have turned to the landscape because men disappoint me:
the trunk of a tree is proud; when the woodmen fell it,
it still has a contained ionic solemnity:
it is a rounded event without the need to tell it.

I have never been compelled to turn away from the dawn
because it carries treason behind its wakened face:
even the horned ram, glowering over the bog hole,
though symbol of evil, will step through the blown grass with
    grace.

Animal, plant, or insect, stone or water,
are, every minute, themselves; they behave by law.
I am not required to discover motives for them,
or strip my heart to forgive the rat in the straw.

I live my best in the landscape, being at ease there;
the only trouble I find I have brought in my hand.
See, I let it fall with a rustle of stems in the nettles,
and never for a moment suppose that they understand.

O COUNTRY PEOPLE

O country people, you of the hill farms,
huddled so in darkness I cannot tell
whether the light across the glen is a star,
or the bright lamp spilling over the sill,
I would be neighbourly, would come to terms
with your existence, but you are so far;
there is a wide bog between us, a high wall.
I've tried to learn the smaller parts of speech
in your slow language, but my thoughts need more
flexible shapes to move in, if I am to reach
into the hearth's red heart across the half-door.

You are coarse to my senses, to my washed skin;
I shall maybe learn to wear dung on my heel,
but the slow assurance, the unconscious discipline
informing your vocabulary of skill,
is beyond my mastery, who have followed a trade
three generations now, at counter and desk;
hand me a rake, and I at once, betrayed,
will shed more sweat than is needed for the task.

If I could gear my mind to the year's round,
take season into season without a break,
instead of feeling my heart bound and rebound
because of the full moon or the first snowflake,
I should have gained something. Your secret is pace.
Already in your company I can keep step,
but alone, involved in a headlong race,
I never know the moment when to stop.

I know the level you accept me on,
like a strange bird observed about the house,
or sometimes seen out flying on the moss
that may tomorrow, or next week, be gone,
liable to return without warning
on a May afternoon and away in the morning.

But we are no part of your world, your way,
as a field or a tree is, or a spring well.
We are not held to you by the mesh of kin;
we must always take a step back to begin,
and there are many things you never tell
because we would not know the things you say.

I recognise the limits I can stretch;
even a lifetime among you should leave me strange,
for I could not change enough, and you will not change;
there'd still be levels neither'd ever reach.
And so I cannot ever hope to become,
for all my good will toward you, yours to me,
even a phrase or a story which will come
pat to the tongue, part of the tapestry
of apt response, at the appropriate time,
like a wise saw, a joke, an ancient rime
used when the last stack's topped at the day's end,
or when the last lint's carted round the bend.

MAN FISH AND BIRD

Bird fish and man
I cannot fly into the sun
but I can carry the sun in my head
I cannot dive cavorting
over and round the submerged rocks and in the water
but the circumambience of space
whether full of water, air or particles of sand,
I can contain
I can also contain it empty.

I cannot sit in that chair
when the man is sitting there
but I can contain the chair, the man sitting
and my sitting where the man is sitting therefore
I am bird fish and man and the circumambience.

This is the first day.

I can carry man fish and bird to the mountain top
I can lie in a dark place and be full of light
I can say to the man be fish and he fins among the firs
I can say to the fish be bird
and it will build a nest beside a crab.

This is the second day.

I can take words to cover
the man fish and bird
I can write the words, writing
Green Man Yellow Fish Red Bird

and the green man is spring
pushing fingers, then his whole hands and wrists
through the wet mould;
and the yellow fish leaps out of the waters
and the darkness becomes dawn;
and the red bird calls the yellow fish back to the sea
and darkness resumes
but the red bird is also my heart crying against the darkness
and may also beak out of the rocks with dawn in its call.

This is the third day.

I can tell the green man I understand him
and ask him to answer my questions
I can feed the yellow fish with the ants' eggs of my affection
letting it lip my palm and vanish away with a swift curve
I can tell the red bird to cry dawn in lonely places
and I can stand lonely and inhabited at the same time
in doubt and in understanding.

This is the fourth day.

When my mind is clenched
I can bid these creatures inhabit the circumambience
but when I sleep entering the darkness
that darkness becomes their circumambience and
  their liberty
and the green man is my father
and the yellow fish far back in my generations
and the red bird is a moment I had forgotten
a moment of grief or humiliation.

And this is the fifth day.

I can come down from the mountain and ask the people
Have you heard the answers of the Green Man
Have you seen the Yellow Fish pass this way
Did you feed it and speed it on its journey
Did the Red Bird cry to you in your loneliness.

And many will say No we saw or heard nothing.

And others will say The Man who answered was white
and the Fish you call Yellow was not yellow: it was
the colour of this handkerchief or this flag
and the Bird was most certainly not Red
A red bird is a monster. The Bird
was yellow Not the Fish. Indeed
it was not a bird at all it was
a feathered serpent or a cockatrice.

And some will say Yes we heard the answers
the Green Man made but fail to understand them
and the Yellow Fish passed so quickly we caught only
  a glimpse
and the Red Bird cried yesterday but across the frontier
tomorrow it may cry nearer

and two will say Yes we heard the Green Man
answering the Green Man's questions
but the Yellow Fish gave no hint of his intentions
and the Red Bird flew down out of a piece of Chinese
   needlework.
And one will say Hallo Green Man
and, Yellow Fish you have returned already
and Red Bird I bid you welcome. You are needed
to cry light against the shadow here.

This is the sixth day.

When my mind can no longer because of age
or mishap clench within itself the circumambience
and the man and the fish and the bird
I shall lie down in shadow which will deepen into
   darkness
and the man will sit in his chair
and I shall sit in his chair and be in his mind
and the green man of the split sod
and the yellow fish will turn and turn in swift curves
in the globe of his skull
peering out of his eyes in passing
and the red bird will fly shouting out of his mouth.

This is the seventh day
Man Fish and Bird.

THE COLONY

First came the legions, then the colonists,
provincials, landless citizens, and some
camp-followers of restless generals
content now only with the least of wars.
Among this rabble, some to feel more free
beyond the ready whim of Caesar's fist;
for conscience' sake the best of these, but others
because their debts had tongues, one reckless man,
a tax absconder with a sack of coin.

With these, young law clerks skilled with chart and stylus,
their boxes crammed with lease-scrolls duly marked
with distances and names, to be defined
when all was mapped.
                When they'd surveyed the land,
they gave the richer tillage, tract by tract,
from the great captains down to men-at-arms,
some of the sprawling rents to be retained
by Caesar's mistresses in their far villas.

We planted little towns to garrison
the heaving country, heaping walls of earth
and keeping all our cattle close at hand;
then, thrusting north and west, we felled the trees,
selling them off the foothills, at a stroke
making quick profits, smoking out the nests
of the barbarian tribesmen, clan by clan,
who hunkered in their blankets, biding chance,
till, unobserved, they slither down and run
with torch and blade among the frontier huts

when guards were nodding, or when shining corn
bade sword-hand grip the sickle. There was once
a terrible year when, huddled in our towns,
my people trembled as the beacons ran
from hill to hill across the countryside,
calling the dispossessed to lift their standards.
There was great slaughter then, man, woman, child,
with fire and pillage of our timbered houses;
we had to build in stone for ever after.

That terror dogs us; back of all our thought
the threat behind the dream, those beacons flare,
and we run headlong, screaming in our fear;
fear quickened by the memory of guilt
for we began the plunder – naked men
still have their household gods and holy places,
and what a people loves it will defend.
We took their temples from them and forbade them,
for many years, to worship their strange idols.
They gathered secret, deep in the dripping glens,
chanting their prayers before a lichened rock.

We took the kindlier soils. It had been theirs,
this patient, temperate, slow, indifferent,
crop-yielding, crop-denying, in-neglect-
quickly-returning-to-the-nettle-and-bracken,
sodden and friendly land. We took it from them.
We laboured hard and stubborn, draining, planting,
till half the country took its shape from us.

Only among the hills with hare and kestrel
will you observe what once this land was like
before we made it fat for human use –
all but the forests, all but the tall trees –
I could invent a legend of those trees,
and how their creatures, dryads, hamadryads,
fled from the copses, hid in thorny bushes,
and grew a crooked and malignant folk,
plotting and waiting for a bitter revenge
on their despoilers. So our troubled thought
is from enchantments of the old tree magic,
but I am not a sick and haunted man …

Teams of the tamer natives we employed
to hew and draw, but did not call them slaves.
Some say this was our error. Others claim
we were too slow to make them citizens;
we might have made them Caesar's bravest legions.
This is a matter for historians,
or old beards in the Senate to wag over,
not pertinent to us these many years.

But here and there the land was poor and starved,
which, though we mapped, we did not occupy,
leaving the natives, out of laziness
in our demanding it, to hold unleased
the marshy quarters, fens, the broken hills,
and all the rougher places where the whin
still thrust from limestone with its cracking pods.

They multiplied and came with open hands,
begging a crust because their land was poor,
and they were many; squatting at our gates,
till our towns grew and threw them hovelled lanes
which they inhabit still. You may distinguish,
if you were schooled with us, by pigmentation,
by cast of features or by turn of phrase,
or by the clan names on them which are they,
among the faces moving in the street.
They worship Heaven strangely, having rites
we snigger at, are known as superstitious,
cunning by nature, never to be trusted,
given to dancing and a kind of song
seductive to the ear, a whining sorrow.
Also they breed like flies. The danger's there;
when Caesar's old and lays his sceptre down,
we'll be a little people, well outnumbered.

Some of us think our leases have run out
but dig square heels in, keep the roads repaired;
and one or two loud voices would restore
the rack, the yellow patch, the curfewed ghetto.
Most try to ignore the question, going their way,
glad to be living, sure that Caesar's word
is Caesar's bond for legions in our need.
Among us, some, beguiled by their sad music,
make common cause with the natives, in their hearts
hoping to win a truce when the tribes assert
their ancient right and take what once was theirs.
Already from other lands the legions ebb
and men no longer know the Roman peace.

Alone, I have a harder row to hoe:
I think these natives human, think their code,
though strange to us, and farther from the truth,
only a little so – to be redeemed
if they themselves rise up against the spells
and fears their celibates surround them with.
I find their symbols good, as such, for me,
when I walk in dark places of the heart;
but name them not to be misunderstood.
I know no vices they monopolise,
if we allow the forms by hunger bred,
the sores of old oppression, the deep skill
in all evasive acts, the swaddled minds,
admit our load of guilt – I mourn the trees
more than as symbol – and would make amends
by fraternising, by small friendly gestures,
hoping by patient words I may convince
my people and this people we are changed
from the raw levies which usurped the land,
if not to kin, to co-inhabitants,
as goat and ox may graze in the same field
and each gain something from proximity;
for we have rights drawn from the soil and sky;
the use, the pace, the patient years of labour,
the rain against the lips, the changing light,
the heavy clay-sucked stride, have altered us;
we would be strangers in the Capitol;
this is our country also, nowhere else;
and we shall not be outcast on the world.

THE STOAT

Walking in the warmest afternoon
this year has yielded yet, through slopes of whin
that made the shadows luminous, and filled
the slow air with its fragrance, we went down
a narrow track, stone-littered, under trees
which with new leaf and opening bud contrived
to offer a green commentary on light;
and as we wondered silent, stone by stone,
on lavish spring, a sudden volley broke,
a squealing terror ripped through twig and briar,
as a small rabbit pawing at the air
and stilting quickly thrust full into view,
clenched on its rump a dark-eyed stoat was viced,
shaped in its naked purpose to destroy.
We stopped. I stepped across. Before a stick
could fall in mercy, its harsh grip released,
the crouched stoat vanished, and the rabbit ran
whimpering and yelping into the thick grass.
Something had happened to the afternoon;
the neighbourly benevolence of spring
was shattered with that cast of violence;
and as we turned to follow the steep track,
it seemed no inconsistent codicil,
that in the mud a broken shell should loll
in equal speckled parts, and on a stone,
a little yolk, a golden sixpence, lay,
a fallen sun in a wrecked universe.

THE WATCHERS

We crouched and waited as the day ebbed off
and the close birdsong dwindled point by point,
nor daring the indulgence of a cough
nor the jerked protest of a weary joint;
and when our sixty minutes had run by
and lost themselves in the declining light
we heard the warning snuffle and the sly
scuffle of mould, and, instantly, the white
long head thrust through the sighing undergrowth,
and the grey badger scrambled into view,
eager to frolic carelessly, yet loth
to trust the air his greedy nostrils drew;
awhile debated with each distant sound,
then, settling into confidence, began
to scratch his tough-haired side, to sniff the ground
without the threat of that old monster, man.
And as we watched him, gripped in our surprise,
that moment suddenly began to mean
more than a badger, and a row of eyes,
a stony brook, a leafy ditch between.
It was as if another nature came
close to my knowledge, but could not be known;
yet if I tried to call it by its name
would start, alarmed, and instantly be gone.

HEDGEHOG

Outside my senses, known as printed words,
as tinted woodcut half a life ago,
the crouching hedgehog on the roadside sward
epitomised in spike and panting flank
the world of things I know and do not know.

True to the legend, when I threatened it,
the ball defensive coiled before my eyes;
the twitching snout, the small pathetic hands
withdrew and left me utterly expelled,
no longer free of Adam's paradise.

Patient I waited till the fear was spent,
and watched the waking from that little death,
a fellow creature native to my sod,
nervous and mortal, meant to be alive,
and eager for the purposes of breath.

RITE, LUBITAVISH, GLENAAN

Above my door the rushy cross,
the turf upon my hearth,
for I am of the Irishry
by nurture and by birth.

So let no patriot decry
or Kelt dispute my claim,
for I have found the faith was here
before Saint Patrick came.

The healing well by Rachray's cliff
that answers to the tide,
the blessing of the gentle bush
deep in my pulse abide.

Before men swung the crooked scythe,
I flung my hook with care,
and from the stook-lined harvest field
bore off the plaited hare.

And yesterday as I came down
where Oisin's gravestones stand,
the holly branch with berries hung
thrust upright in my hand.

THE OWL

With quiet step and careful breath
we rubbered over grass and stone,
seeking that soft light-feathered bird
among the trees where it had flown.
The twisting road ran down beside
a straggling wood of ash and beech;
between us and the shadowed trees
a wire fence topped the whin-spiked ditch.
We stood and gazed: the only stir
of dry leaves in the topmost boughs;
the only noise now, far away,
the cawing of the roosting crows.
And as we watched in waning light,
our clenched attention pinned upon
that empty corner of the wood,
it seemed the quiet bird had gone.

Then when the light had ebbed to dusk
you moved a hand and signalled me:
I saw the little pointed ears
beside a tall and narrow tree.
A further signal, and I moved
in wide half-circle to surprise
that little feathered sheaf of life
that watched you watch with steady eyes.
But when I came by easy stealth,
at last, within a yard or two
the brown bird spread enormous wings
and rose and quietly withdrew.

And we were left to carry home
a sense no mortal will devised,
that, for one instant out of time,
we had been seen and recognised.

THE MUNICIPAL GALLERY
REVISITED, OCTOBER 1954

Brisk from the autumn of the sunlit square,
to overbrim a day already full,
because some exhibition drew me there,
the mannered essays of the latest school,
I stumbled into history unaware,
pausing a moment in the vestibule,
among the crowding presences again,
facing disarmed the stone and metal men:

O'Leary brooding in his long bronze beard,
out of the saga now, a king remote;
the tense faun, Shaw, by Rodin's marble spared
the pitiful declension of his thought:
and Stephens only known as overheard
billowed on ether, or as what he wrote,
a small grimacing urchin looking lost,
too wry and various for any ghost:

George Russell, then, my fellow countryman,
a lad this, as of seventy years ago;
you could not tell from this slight beardless one
that this was he who, in day's afterglow,
saw timeless creatures on gay errands run,
for there's no lettered label here to show
what scale or scope this stripling promised us;
no note here, either, of the sculptor, Hughes:

and this, the bold-jawed orator in bronze,
torch of rebellion, fanned by roaring crowds –
clutching my father's hand, I saw him once,
when heaven seemed scarcely higher than the clouds,
muster his dispossessed battalions –
who guttered his bright flame in smoky feuds;
but there's no name here either: you must guess
what passions forged these features with what stress:

another, named at least, a comely face
scorched to the skull and ardour of a saint,
a legend she, of time-surmounting grace:
verse ambers her beyond all scathe or taint,
and she's safe there; though in this silent place
false patination of the flaking paint,
indifferent as weather, has defaced
what should long since have been in metal cast.

And as I moved among these images,
nameless or named, still emblems of the power
that wrought a nation out of bitterness,
and gave its history one triumphant hour,
my heart, dejected, wondered which of these
may hold a meaning that will long endure,
for, see, before me, threatening, immense,
the creeping haircracks of indifference.

OSSIAN'S GRAVE, LUBITAVISH, COUNTY ANTRIM

We stood and pondered on the stones
whose plan displays their pattern still;
the small blunt arc, and, sill by sill,
the pockets stripped of shards and bones.

The legend has it, Ossian lies
beneath this landmark on the hill,
asleep till Fionn and Oscar rise
to summon his old bardic skill
in hosting their last enterprise.

This, stricter scholarship denies,
declares this megalithic form
millennia older than his time –
if such lived ever, out of rime –
was shaped beneath Sardinian skies,
was coasted round the capes of Spain,
brought here through black Biscayan storm,
to keep men's hearts in mind of home
and its tall Sun God, wise and warm,
across the walls of toppling foam,
against this twilight and the rain.

I cannot tell; would ask no proof;
let either story stand for true,
as heart or head shall rule. Enough
that, our long meditation done,
as we paced down the broken lane
by the dark hillside's holly trees,
a great white horse with lifted knees
came stepping past us, and we knew
his rider was no tinker's son.

THE FRONTIER

At the frontier the long train slows to a stop:
small men in uniform drift down the corridor,
thumb passports, or withdraw for consultation;
the customs officers chalk the bags and leave us to shut them.

We pass here into another allegiance,
expect new postage stamps, new prices, manifestoes,
and brace ourselves for the change. But the landscape does
   not alter;
we had already entered these mountains an hour ago.

JACOB AND THE ANGEL

I wrestled with my father in my dream,
holding my ground though he strove powerfully,
then suddenly remembered who we were,
and why we need not struggle, he and I;
thereat desisted. Now the meaning's clear;
I will not pause to struggle with my past,
locked in an angry posture with a ghost,
but, striding forward, trust the shrunken thigh.

AN IRISHMAN IN COVENTRY

A full year since, I took this eager city,
the tolerance that laced its blatant roar,
its famous steeples and its web of girders,
as image of the state hope argued for,
and scarcely flung a bitter thought behind me
on all that flaws the glory and the grace
which ribbons through the sick, guilt-clotted legend
of my creed-haunted, godforsaken race.
My rhetoric swung round from steel's high promise
to the precision of the well-gauged tool,
tracing the logic in the vast glass headlands,
the clockwork horse, the comprehensive school.

Then, sudden, by occasion's chance concerted,
in enclave of my nation, but apart,
the jigging dances and the lilting fiddle
stirred the old rage and pity in my heart.
The faces and the voices blurring round me,
the strong hands long familiar with the spade,
the whiskey-tinctured breath, the pious buttons,
called up a people endlessly betrayed
by our own weakness, by the wrongs we suffered
in that long twilight over bog and glen,
by force, by famine and by glittering fables
which gave us martyrs when we needed men,
by faith which had no charity to offer
by poisoned memory, and by ready wit,
with poverty corroded into malice,
to hit and run and howl when it is hit.

This is our fate: eight hundred years' disaster,
crazily tangled as the Book of Kells;
the dream's distortion and the land's division,
the midnight raiders and the prison cells.
Yet like Lir's children banished to the waters
our hearts still listen for the landward bells.

WHIT MONDAY

The small girls hurried to the hilltop church,
their confirmation dresses fluttering
in the late sun. Before the shadowed porch
neat-fingered mothers knotted lace and string
and pinned each floral coronet in place;
while the dark-suited fathers stood apart,
pride and affection on each polished face:
it seemed as though some play were poised to start,
when the last swift had scoured the humming air.

Yet this was Poland, and the time was now;
and I, who pray too seldom, felt a prayer
take all my will, that providence allow,
or dialectic, or whatever name
men put upon time's enginery, permit
this scene to re-enact itself, the same,
so long as any heart finds grace in it.

MY GRANDMOTHER'S GARTER

I never really liked my mother's mother;
she was too stiff and hard:
a single kindly word from those puckered lips
I never heard.

Slim, handsome, straight as a rush, her soft hair white,
smooth-skinned and fresh of cheek,
with purple ribbons threaded in jet-beaded cap,
always in black;

those who knew her acknowledged her the regent
of her grim Methodist God.
The little lead figures on the drawing-room piano
would, when you blew on them, nod.

Possessive of her house and six grown-up children,
she worshipped her eldest son,
but found the fast anchor of her long widowhood
in the second, John.

She faulted and quarrelled with every servant girl
until, in tears, she left,
suspected of trying to seduce the master,
accused of theft.

After twenty years he married, escaped and died
untimely, that good man.
So, when the house was sold and the young widow
    pensioned,
her travels began.

Each daughter's home, in turn, became her haven,
till restlessness set in.
The disagreements flared to rows; she packed her trunks,
and moved again,

keeping her children in perpetual turmoil,
a disruptive element,
leaving a trail of misunderstanding and malice
everywhere she went.

Yet she always had a pouch in her garter,
stuffed with snippets of clipped verse;
Tennyson, Whittier, Longfellow, George MacDonald,
the guineas in her purse.

And when at last she died there was scant mourning;
her eldest son already dead,
the family had poured its load of sorrow
over that noble head.

Yet, though I did not like her, nor she me, swearing
I'd come to a bad end,
remembering that satin pouch of poems,
I clasp her bony hand.

APRIL AWAKE

Lark-bright the air; the light
from leafing hedge and willow
was faceted with white
of blackthorn and whin-yellow.

The climbing sun made light
of the purple-shadowed furrow;
white was the lime, and white
the horse that dragged the harrow.

FOOTING TURF

Footing turf on high Barard, the hip
of that long mountain, Trostan, it was cold
and wet, and every hair on sleeve or wrist
was globed with water, and the tangled grass
shod each chill foot with moisture. The whole world
was narrowed to a little dripping cave
walled by the weather and the bleat of sheep,
but when a gust of wind blew off the roof
the sky was clear and bright, and miles away,
down the landslope towards the quiet sea,
the day-long sun shone on the haymakers.

SUNSET OVER GLENAAN

As the vague sun that wrapped the mellow day
in a grey haze hangs red, about to drop
behind the western mountain rim, I stop
to name the peaks along their dark array,
for these are more than mountains shouldered clear
into the sharp star-pointed atmosphere,
into the sunset. They mark out and bound
the utmost limits of my chosen ground;
beyond them, and beyond the heather and moss
that only lonely roads and shepherds cross,
lie the fat valleys of another folk
who swarmed and settled when the clansmen broke
and limped defeated to the woody glens.

These inland Planter folk are skilled in toil,
their days, their holdings, so well husbanded,
economy has drilled the very soil
into a dulled prosperity that year
by reckoned year continues so; but here
the people have such history of wars,
that every hilltop wears its cairn of dead
and ancient memories of turbulence,
clan names persisting in each rocky stead.
They take life easier on their hillside farms,
with time to pause for talk, remembering
they'll be outlasted by the marching stars,
and, though there may be virtue still in charms,
no man dare be too sure of anything.

My breed is Planter also. I can shew
the grey and crooked headstones row on row
in a rich country mastered long ago
by stubborn farmers from across the sea,
whose minds and hands were rich in husbandry,
and who, when their slow blood was running thin,
crowded in towns for warmth, and bred me in
the clay-red city with the white horse on the wall,
the jangling steeples, and the green-domed hall.

Inheritor of these, I also share
the nature of this legendary air,
reaching a peace and speech I do not find
familiarly among my kin and kind.
Maybe, at some dark level, grown aware
of our old load of guilt, I shrink afraid,
and seek the false truce of a renegade;
or is it that the unchristened heart of man
still hankers for the little friendly clan
that lives as native as the lark or hare?

And though to keep my brain and body alive
I need the honey of the city hive,
I also need for nurture of the heart
the rowan berries and the painted cart,
the bell at noon, the scythesman in the corn,
the cross of rushes, and the fairy thorn.

MAY ALTAR

In every farmhouse through the thorn-white Glens
this is the season when the little girls
put on white dresses, veils and tinsel wreaths,
and flock to Confirmation. Three swift years
it is since Rose was dressed and photographed;
now her two younger sisters are received
into that faith and haven I salute
but sheer away from. In the smoky kitchen
the little posies on the cupboard's top,
pale lady's-smock and blowsy rhododendron,
are set out neatly in the six glass jars,
and in the midst there stands, on this May altar,
the chipped and battered statue of the Virgin,
but my heart hankers for the pagan thorn
that none dare break a spray from and bring in.

THE BALLAD

I named a ballad round a sparking fire,
the children squatting on the hobs, the mother
busy with cans; the husband turned his knife
in the pipe-ash and said: 'I knew the man
that wrote it years ago. He was a tramp
and beat about the roads here.' Then he spoke
a stanza from it in the singsong way
that things are learnt by heart and not by head.

I queried further. Aye, the names were right.
There was a smiddy once, and yon's the place
they saw the Yeos come riding from, and ran
to warn the blacksmith. Then the mother told
how once the tramp begged shelter in the house,
and how her mother sat with him all night
beside the warm fire singing song for song.

The father nodded, knowing the tale well;
the clustered children listened with bright eyes,
and so the ballad and its poet started
on five new journeys through the mounting years:
and I whose care is set on riming words
felt a sharp jag of envy and of pride.

THE WAKE

We snicked the latch where one was dead,
constrained by ancient courtesy;
the open coffin on the bed
shewed us the man we'd come to see.

We gave our greetings to the gloom;
I found a seat against the wall;
my wife was hustled to 'the room'
where women were foregathered all.

Since turf and wick gave feeble light,
the crouching shapes seemed much the same;
with anxious ear and questing sight
I sought to join each shape and name.

Of stock and weather was the talk,
of harvests fabulously great –
the distances men used to walk –
the dangers of our pampered state.

Then one would rise and say good night,
and one who stood would take his chair;
the smoking turf would flicker bright
with each fresh gust of chilly air.

Then suddenly the only sound
would be of crickets at the grate;
and James would reach and hand around
tobacco on a dinner plate.

THE BELL

Here in the hill-rimmed house
where the angelus bell is heard,
when the wind's from the south or west,
as clear as the nearest bird,

today, because the wind
is strong from another airt,
and the rain beats loud on the earth,
you must listen deep in your heart

for the sound of that baffled bell;
yet the chaffinch on the thorn
still offers his ripple of notes
to the tips of the brairding corn.

THE HILL-FARM

My errand brought me once again
along the steep road, down the lane;
and through the long and stumbling dark
there was no cry, no welcome bark
announced my nearing. All was still
from lamp in glen to star on hill.
The door was shut, but curtained light
thrust muffled challenge to the night.
Then at the porch I stopped and stood
to muster courage to intrude,
for, as I paused, I overheard
the rise and fall of rhythmic word,
a voice, the mother's giving clear
the rosary, the evening prayer,
and, mumbling on a lower key,
the voices of the family
responding and repeating, each
with adult or with childish speech,
the invocations running on,
with, now and then, a smothered yawn.

At each Hail Mary, Full of Grace,
I pictured every friendly face,
clenched in devotion of a kind
alien to my breed and mind,
easy as breathing, natural
as birds that fly, as leaves that fall;
yet with a sense that I still stood
far from that faith-based certitude,
here in the vast enclosing night,
outside its little ring of light.

GLOSS, ON THE DIFFICULTIES OF TRANSLATION

Across Lock Laig
the yellow-billed blackbird
whistles from the blossomed whin.

Not, as you might expect,
a Japanese poem, although
it has the seventeen
syllables of the haiku.
Ninth-century Irish, in fact,
from a handbook on metrics,
the first written reference
to my native place.

In forty years of verse
I have not inched much further.
I may have matched the images;
but the intricate wordplay
of the original – assonance,
rime, alliteration –
is beyond my grasp.

To begin with, I should
have to substitute
golden for *yellow*
and *gorse* for *whin*,
this last is the word we use
on both sides of Belfast Lough.

AN ULSTERMAN

This is my country. If my people came
from England here four centuries ago,
the only trace that's left is in my name.
Kilmore, Armagh, no other sod can show
the weathered stone of our first burying.
Born in Belfast, which drew the landless in,
that river-straddling, hill-rimmed town, I cling
to the inflexions of my origin.

Though creed-crazed zealots and the ignorant crowd,
long-nurtured, never checked, in ways of hate,
have made our streets a byword of offence,
this is my country, never disavowed.
When it is fouled, shall I not remonstrate?
My heritage is not their violence.

THE DILEMMA

Born is this island, maimed by history
and creed-infected, by my father taught
the stubborn habit of unfettered thought,
I dreamed, like him, all people should be free.
So, while my logic steered me well outside
that ailing church which claims dominion
over the questing spirit, I denied
all credence to the state by rebels won
from a torn nation, rigged to guard their gain,
though they assert their love of liberty,
which craft has narrowed to a fear of Rome.
So, since this ruptured country is my home,
it long has been my bitter luck to be
caught in the crossfire of their false campaign.

STREET NAMES

I hear the street names on the radio
and map reported bomb or barricade:
this was my childhood's precinct, and I know
how such streets look, down to the very shade
of brick, of paintwork on each door and sill,
what school or church nearby one might attend,
if there's a chance to glimpse familiar hill
between the chimneys where the grey slates end.

Yet I speak only of appearances,
a stage unpeopled, not the tragic play:
though actual faces of known families
flash back across the gap of fifty years;
can these be theirs, the children that today
rage in the fetters of their fathers' fears?

THE COASTERS

You coasted along
to larger houses, gadgets, more machines,
to golf and weekend bungalows,
caravans when the children were small,
the Mediterranean, later, with the wife.

You did not go to church often,
weddings were special;
but you kept your name on the books
against eventualities;
and the parson called, or the curate.

You showed a sense of responsibility,
with subscriptions to worthwhile causes
and service in voluntary organisations;
and, anyhow, this did the business no harm,
no harm at all.
Relations were improving. A good
useful life. You coasted along.

You even had a friend or two of the other sort,
coasting too: your ways ran parallel.
Their children and yours seldom met, though,
being at different schools.
You visited each other, decent folk with a sense
of humour. Introduced, even, to
one of their clergy. And then you smiled
in the looking glass, admiring, a
little moved by, your broadmindedness.

Your father would never have known
one of them. Come to think of it,
when you were young, your own home was never
visited by one of the other sort.

Relations were improving. The annual processions
began to look rather like folk festivals.

When that noisy preacher started,
he seemed old-fashioned, a survival.
Later you remarked on his vehemence,
a bit on the rough side.
But you said, admit it, you said in the club,
'You know, there's something in what he says.'

And you who seldom had time to read a book,
what with reports and the colour supplements,
denounced censorship.
And you who never had an adventurous thought
were positive that the church of the other sort
vetoes thought.
And you, who simply put up with marriage
for the children's sake, deplored
the attitude of the other sort
to divorce.
You coasted along.
And all the time, though you never noticed,
the old lies festered;
the ignorant became more thoroughly infected;
there were gains, of course;
you never saw any go barefoot.

The government permanent, sustained
by the regular plebiscites of loyalty.
You always voted but never
put a sticker on the car;
a card in the window
would not have been seen from the street.
Faces changed on the posters, names too, often,
but the same families, the same class of people.
A minister once called you by your first name.
You coasted along
and the sores suppurated and spread.

Now the fever is high and raging;
who would have guessed it, coasting along?
The ignorant-sick thresh about in delirium
and tear at the scabs with dirty fingernails.
The cloud of infection hangs over the city,
a quick change of wind and it
might spill over the leafy suburbs.
You coasted too long.

BLACK AND WHITE

A blackbird flew to a hawthorn bush
and brushed a flutter of petals down;
they tumbled and turned like a flurry of snow
and settled slow on the waiting stone.

And, if that blackbird, all summer through,
could sing so long as there's light to see,
he would never fling a song as bright
as that lyric flight from the hawthorn tree.

THE STORM

My gate is swinging by one hinge
twigs are scattered on the pavement
the withered chrysanthemums
have daubed themselves with mud
the lake has a feathery edge
the old grasses make a dry sound
and I think of my Chinese friend
on a ship going home.

FROM THE CHINESE OF WANG LI SHI

The Mourne Mountains like a team of bears
tumbling into the sea,
the embroidered fields like a monk's patched cloak
spreading their skirts to every door,
the peasants leisurely allowing
the chickens and dogs to wander at will
the bare trees standing silent
entangle the stranger's dream.

CHINESE FLUTEPLAYER

The small bronze figure lips a silent flute,
and stillness spreads about him like a lake;
he stands there out of time, and once you look
you are involved, released from mortal state,
because all sense is channelled into sight.
See how light strikes and strokes his rounded brow
and pauses on his dreaming-lidded eyes –
this shell of metal sings for ever now.

EMILY DICKINSON

When I, the easy one, was hurt
as never hurt before
I fumbled back through files of verse
for one who suffered more.

But all the poets' proverbs slept
as dry as my swept brain,
save that sweet witch who knew at once
my idiom of pain.

SCISSORS FOR A ONE-ARMED TAILOR

The beggar, when I hurried to the door,
began the usual whine, this lack of pence
no fault of his; just luck, this being poor.
I told him that he needed no defence.

I dared to venture: did he play or sing,
or maybe write great poems on events?
Aye, all of that; but more than anything,
he'd greater notions than ten parliaments.

He mentioned some. I found a cast-off shirt
and fumbled coppers for his doss-house bed,
his white beard grey with thirty counties' dirt
and seventeen inventions in his head.

GREY AND WHITE

Grey sea, grey sky
two things are bright;
the gull-white foam,
the gull, foam-white.

SKYPIECE

After a blatant dawn of red and gold,
the wind wiped off the clouds and left the sky
as clear as a glass of water and as cold,
and the dead moon was like a blind man's eye.

I WRITE FOR ...

I write for my own kind,
I do not pitch my voice
that every phrase be heard
by those who have no choice:
their quality of mind
must be withdrawn and still,
as moth that answers moth
across a roaring hill.

THE SEARCH
for Shirley and Darryl

We left the western island to live among strangers
in a city older by centuries
than the market town which we had come from
where the slow river spills out between green hills
and gulls perch on the bannered poles.

It is a hard responsibility to be a stranger;
to hear your speech sounding at odds with your
    neighbours';
holding your tongue from quick comparisons;
remembering that you are a guest in the house.

Often you will regret the voyage,
wakening in the dark night to recall that other place
or glimpsing the moon rising and recollecting
that it is also rising over named hills,
shining on known waters.

But sometimes the thought
that you have not come away from, but returned,
to this older place whose landmarks are yours also,
occurs when you look down a long street remarking
the architectural styles or move through a landscape
with wheat ripening in large fields.

Yet you may not rest here, having come back,
for this is not your abiding place, either.

The authorities declare that in former days
the western island was uninhabited,
just as where you reside now was once tundra,
and what you seek may be no more than
a broken circle of stones on a rough hillside, somewhere.

FROM THE TIBETAN

In my native province when I was young
the lamas were presumed to be dishonest,
not because they were more wicked than the rest
but their calling gave them more scope.

They were not expected to be philosophers
or poets, for they were not educated persons;
theories were as inconceivable as books
in their satchels. All they were asked
was to provide certain familiar noises
on fixed occasions of the calendar,
spinning the wheels with ritual fervour
and chanting of 'The Emperor's Tunic'
and 'The Great Wall of China'.

For the rest of their time it was anticipated
that they should work hard rewarding their families,
promoting their nephews, replenishing their stores,
and accepting presents from contractors.
Traditionally, all this was to be done with a show
of cordiality, with handclasps, salutes,
conspicuous finger-signals and audible passwords:
the effect which it was desired to produce
being that of reluctant necessity
for complicated manoeuvre.

Now I am older and live in the suburbs of the capital,
I find that the lamas here are very much the same,
save that the rewarding, promoting, replenishing, is
done on their behalf by a permanent secretariat,
leaving them more time to devote to the illusion
of exercising power: this forces them to acquire
a more sophisticated vocabulary; indeed,
one or two of them have written books:
in my native province this
would have been looked upon with disfavour,
for we are a simple people.

ET TU IN ARCADIA VIXISTI
for Roberta

You woke me, rising – this in Paris once –
I watched you stepping – thirty years ago –
to the long window. Many such we've since
unshuttered back from narrow streets below,
but on no more than stir of wheel or foot –
as, finger-signalled, following, I stood
beside you, heeding, drifting up, a flute-
like music, blown through the clean hollow wood,
while, leaning, a dark lad against the wall
played to the splay of goats about his knees,
strayed, so it seemed, from classic pastoral,
an instant's magic – never ours in Greece,
when, later, older, or in Sicily,
we stood, at dawn, beside the tideless sea.

THE SCAR
for Padraic Fiacc

There's not a chance now that I might recover
one syllable of what that sick man said,
tapping upon my great-grandmother's shutter,
and begging, I was told, a piece of bread;
for on his tainted breath there hung infection
rank from the cabins of the stricken west,
the spores from black potato-stalks, the spittle
mottled with poison in his rattling chest;
but she who, by her nature, quickly answered,
accepted in return the famine-fever;
and that chance meeting, that brief confrontation,
conscribed me of the Irishry for ever.

Though much I cherish lies outside their vision,
and much they prize I have no claim to share,
yet in that woman's death I found my nation;
the old wound aches and shews its fellow scar.

MARY HAGAN, ISLANDMAGEE, 1919

She wore high sea-boots and a wave-dowsed skirt,
a man's cloth cap, a jersey, her forearms freckled,
wind-roughened her strong face; with the men
she hauled the boat up, harsh upon the shingle,
and as they hauled they called out to each other,
she coarse as the rest. A skinny twelve-year-old,
pale from the city, watched this marvellous
creature, large-eyed, from my sun-warmed boulder.

I cannot remember her at any time
tossing the lapped hay, urging home the cattle,
or stepping out on a Sunday: she exists
in that one posture, knuckles on the gunwale,
the great boots crackling on the bladderwrack;
one with Grace Darling, one with Granuaile.

THE KING'S HORSES

After fifty years, nearly, I remember,
living then in a quiet leafy suburb,
waking in the darkness, made aware
of a continuous irregular noise,
and groping to the side window to discover
the shadow-shapes which made that muffled patter
passing across the end of our avenue,
the black trees and the streetlights shuttering
a straggle of flowing shadows, endless, of horses.

Gypsies they could have been, or tinkers maybe,
mustering to some hosting of their clans,
or horse-dealers heading their charges to the docks,
timed to miss the day's traffic and alarms;
a migration the newspapers had not foretold;
some battle's ragged finish, dream repeated;
the last of an age retreating, withdrawing,
leaving us beggared, bereft
of the proud nodding muzzles, the nervous bodies;
gone from us the dark men with their ancient skills of
saddle and stirrup, of bridle and breeding.

It was an end, I was sure, but an end of what
I never could tell. It was never reported;
but the echoing hooves persisted. Years after,
in a London hotel in the grey dawn
a serious man concerned with certain duties,
I heard again the metal clatter of hooves staccato and
hurriedly rose to catch a glimpse of my horses, but the
pace and beat were utterly different:
I saw by the men astride these were the King's horses
going about the King's business, never mine.

CULTRA MANOR:
THE ULSTER FOLK MUSEUM
for Renee and John

After looking at the enlarged photographs
of obsolete rural crafts, the bearded man
winnowing, the women in long skirts
at their embroidery,
the objects on open display, the churn,
the snuff-mill, the dogskin float,
in the Manor House galleries,
we walked among the trees to the half-dozen
re-erected workshops and cottages
transported from the edge of our region,
tidy and white in the mild April sun.

Passing between the archetypal round pillars
with the open five-barred gate,
my friend John said:
'What they need now, somewhere about here,
is a field for the faction fights.'

NEITHER AN ELEGY
NOR A MANIFESTO

for the people of my province
and the rest of Ireland

Bear in mind these dead:
I can find no plainer words.
I dare not risk using
that loaded word, Remember,
for your memory is a cruel web
threaded from thorn to thorn across
a hedge of dead bramble, heavy
with pathetic atomies.

I cannot urge or beg you
to pray for anyone or anything,
for prayer in this green island
is tarnished with stale breath,
worn smooth and characterless
as an old flagstone, trafficked
with journeys no longer credible
to lost destinations.

The careful words of my injunction
are unrhetorical, as neutral
and unaligned as any I know:
they propose no more than thoughtful response;
they do not pound with drum-beats
of patriotism, loyalty, martyrdom.

So I say only: bear in mind
those men and lads killed in the streets;
but do not differentiate between
those deliberately gunned down
and those caught by unaddressed bullets:
such distinctions are not relevant.

Bear in mind the skipping child hit
by the anonymous ricochet;
the man shot at his own fireside
with his staring family round him;
the elderly woman
making tea for the firemen
when the wall collapsed;
and the garrulous neighbours at the bar
when the bomb exploded near them;
the gesticulating deaf-mute stilled
by the soldier's rifle in the town square;
and the policeman dismembered
by the booby-trap in the car.

I might have recited a pitiful litany
of the names of all the dead:
but these could effectively be presented
only in small batches,
like a lettered tablet in a village church,
valid while everyone knew everyone,
or longer, where a family name persists.

Accident, misfortune, disease, coincidence
of genetic factors or social circumstance,
may summon courage, resolution, sympathy,
to whatever level one is engaged.
Natural disasters of lava and hurricane,
famine or flood in far countries, will evoke
compassion for the thin-shanked survivors.

Patriotism has to do with keeping
the country in good heart, the community
ordered with justice and mercy;
these will enlist loyalty and courage often,
and sacrifice, sometimes even martyrdom.
Bear these eventualities in mind also;
they will concern you forever:
but, at this moment, bear in mind these dead.

A BIRTHDAY RHYME
FOR ROBERTA
October 1904–October 1975

For ease of heart and mind
I estimate each stride,
and, lurching forward, find
the landmarks still abide
though senses be decayed,
blurred sight and muffled sound.
Yet yesterday I strayed
on acorn-gravelled ground
to find October true
by each diminished sense,
perpetually new
as grace or innocence.

But now not with me there
picking the coloured leaves,
was she I thought must share
the thistles and the sheaves
when this late harvesting
my husbandry may prove,
as she had shared the spring
and summer of my love.

SUBSTANCE AND SHADOW

There is a bareness in the images
I temper time with in my mind's defence;
they hold their own, their stubborn secrecies;
no use to rage against their reticence:
a gannet's plunge, a heron by a pond,
a last rook homing as the sun goes down,
a spider squatting on a bracken-frond,
and thistles in a cornsheaf's tufted crown,
a boulder on a hillside, lichen-stained,
the sparks of sun on dripping icicles,
their durable significance contained
in texture, colour, shape, and nothing else.
All these are sharp, spare, simple, native to
this small republic I have charted out
as the sure acre where my sense is true,
while round its boundaries sprawl the screes of doubt.

My lamp lights up the kettle on the stove
and throws its shadow on the whitewashed wall,
like some Assyrian profile with, above,
a snake, or bird-prowed helmet crested tall;
but this remains a shadow; when I shift
the lamp or move the kettle it is gone,
the substance and the shadow break adrift
that needed bronze to lock them, bronze or stone.

ENCOUNTER NINETEEN TWENTY

Kicking a ragged ball from lamp to lamp,
in close November dusk, my head well down,
not yet aware the teams had dribbled off,
I collided with a stiffly striding man.

He cursed. I stumbled, glimpsing his sharp face,
his coat brushed open and a rifle held
close to his side. That image has become
the shape of fear that waits each Irish child.

Shock sent each reeling from the light's pale cone;
in shadow since that man moves out to kill;
and I, with thumping heart, from lamp to lamp,
still race to score my sad unchallenged goal.

A MOBILE MOLLUSC

He learned, as a dissenter, he must be
a man who'd never fail to speak his mind,
eager to challenge, readily resigned
to leave all free as he himself was free;
yet, in assertion of that liberty,
still to a stance of arrogance inclined,
a mobile mollusc of a special kind
that finds and foots his rock in any sea.

So, snug within his metaphoric shell,
he edged along the indifferent cliffs with care,
the senses sorting out directions well,
not heeding signals he mistrusted from
insistent tides that headed straight for Rome,
Moscow, Peking, New York, or anywhere.

A LOCAL POET

He followed their lilting stanzas
through a thousand columns or more,
and scratched for the splintered couplets
in the cracks on the cottage floor,
for his Rhyming Weavers fell silent
when they flocked through the factory door.

He'd imagined a highway of heroes
and stepped aside on the grass
to let Cuchullain's chariot through,
and the Starry Ploughmen pass;
but he met the Travelling Gunman
instead of the Galloglass.

And so, with luck, for a decade
down the widowed years ahead,
the pension which crippled his courage
will keep him in daily bread,
while he mourns for his mannerly verses
that had left so much unsaid.

FOR A MOMENT OF DARKNESS OVER THE NATIONS

The black cloud
is a happy portent
for dwellers in the drylands
waiting for the monsoon.

You there,
take up your dusty prayer-wheel.
As for me, I shall stand up
and begin the Rain Dance.

THE ROMANTIC

When the first white flakes
fall out of the black Antrim sky
I toboggan across Alaska.

When a friend falls ill
I rehearse the funeral oration;
since I am for completeness,
never having learned to live at ease
with incompleteness.

THE GLENS OF ANTRIM

I've drawn this landscape now for thirty years,
longer, if scribbles count, from lower ground,
as, climbing to the crest of it, I've found
the changing vesture which each season wears,
striding one hillside; how the hour appears
in rain, in snow, or when the valley's drowned
in drifting mist, or with bright blossom crowned,
the whin-gilt peak rebukes the sun's arrears.

And I have drilled my pen to draw each sign
which peoples time and place within this frame
with plough and harrow, reaper, or the line
of stooped men pulling lint, that when the night
draws darkness over you may mark and name
each lonely homestead by its steady light.

THE BLOSSOMED THORN

That lateness of the season here
allows the thorn to blossom now;
in opulent but brief career
each single bough is bent on show.

Once passing with a troubled mind
I saw one bush of all in flower
that had a presence of a kind
my senses had no sequel for.

As gazing at it long I stood,
a strange awareness stirred within,
not of my flesh becoming wood
and stinging where the buds begin,

but of a flowing universe
that poured and streamed towards the tree,
swept with a magnet's silent force
into the One Reality.

The sluicing earth, the rushing sky
seemed thrusting into twig and spray;
to hoard my risked identity
I had to pluck myself away.

A FATHER'S DEATH

It was no vast dynastic fate
when gasp by gasp my father died,
no mourners at the palace gate,
or tall bells tolling slow and wide.

We sat beside the bed; the screen
shut out the hushed, the tiptoe ward,
and now and then we both would lean
to catch what seemed a whispered word.

My mother watched her days drag by,
two score and five the married years,
yet never weakened to a cry
who was so ready with her tears.

Then, when dawn washed the polished floor
and steps and voices woke and stirred
with wheels along the corridor,
my father went without a word.

The sick, the dying, bed by bed,
lay clenched around their own affairs;
that one behind a screen was dead
was someone's grief, but none of theirs.

It was no vast dynastic death,
no nation silent round that throne,
when, letting go his final breath,
a lonely man went out alone.

from SONNETS FOR ROBERTA (1954)

I

How have I served you? I have let you waste
the substance of your summer on my mood;
the image of the woman is defaced,
and some mere chattel-thing of cloth and wood
performs the household rites, while I, content,
mesh the fine words to net the turning thought,
or eke the hours out, gravely diligent,
to drag to sight that which, when it is brought,
is seldom worth the labour, while you wait,
the little loving gestures held at bay,
each mocking moment inappropriate
for pompous duty never stoops to play;
yet sometimes, at a pause, I recognise
the lonely pity in your lifted eyes.

II

If I had given you that love and care
I long have lavished with harsh loyalty
on some blurred concept spun of earth and air
and real only in some bird or tree,
then you had lived in every pulse and tone
and found the meaning in the wine and bread
who have been forced to walk these ways alone,
my dry thoughts droning always on ahead.
Then you had lived as other women live,
warmed by a touch, responsive to a glance,
glad to endure, so that endurance give
the right to share each changing circumstance,
and yet, for all my treason, you were true
to me, as I to something less than you.

A HAPPY BOY

This is the story of a happy boy,
born in this place while yet the century
scarce offered hint we'd not by now enjoy
a tolerant and just society
through wise congruence of our people's choices;
the path seemed clear, and only for a time
would some, deflected by ancestral voices,
posture and mouth in bigot pantomime.

The map dissolves. Familiar town decays.
No man can ever walk these ways again,
blind to the brooding of the coming storm,
and pacing towards apocalyptic days;
and yet his boyish hope was never vain;
if it seems foolish now, it still stands firm.

BALLOONS AND WOODEN GUNS

O it was lovely round that other house
where I was born and lived for thirty years.
Life surged about us. So that time appears,
dull intervals suppressed, in happy shows:
Italian organ-grinders, parrots, bears;
that blind old Happy Jimmy by himself;
the German bands; the Ulster Volunteers
with wooden guns; the women selling delph;
carts with balloons; great horses galloping,
their huge fire-engine brass and funnelled flames;
strung chestnuts every autumn; kites in spring;
girls skipping; slides and snowballs in the snow;
all those activities which bore the names
of May Queen, Kick-the-Tin, and Rally-O.

THE VOLUNTEER

My father's closest brother of his three
trained as an artist, by compulsion made
his living at the lithographic trade.
After adventures, Edinburgh, he
settled in Finchley with his family.
One Bangor holiday I saw him plain,
his tilted boater and his swagger cane,
a smiling man, he shared some jokes with me.

Months after war broke out he wrote to say
he had enlisted by deliberate choice,
not waiting for conscription, lest his boys
might think of that with shame some future day.
I still recall my father's countenance
that day we learned he had been killed in France.

THE MAGICIAN

So Uncle Sam was truly Prospero,
that house his island palace. There I shared
his marvels and his magic. Thence I'd go
with netted rods and jam-jars well prepared,
to pace the tow-path by the drifting stream,
or step through heather for the furtive moth.
I gaped to watch his magic-lantern beam
figure with life the hoisted tablecloth.

His nimble fingers thrilled the mandolin,
or strummed banjo. Once, with a pointed blade
he gouged a fist-sized eagle from tough oak.
He glittered through my days, a paladin
in all accomplished, nature's tricks his trade,
till one sad day, for me that dream-spell broke.

ORCHARD COUNTRY

When my grandfather came to live with us
my past expanded, for he proffered me,
his lively mind so thronged and populous,
an open door to our own history.
That Armagh orchard country. Yea and Nay
of grave believers. How his mother died
of famine-fever caught the strangest way,
for that was not a famished countryside.
How his grandfather chafed the small child's hands,
chill from the snowballs – bringing life to yours
as he recalled. How Mark's, his father's, cures
healed creature's ills. How in those Planter lands
our name is hearth-rolled. Generation, place,
he gave you foothold in the human race.

THE DOCTOR'S BAG

Old Doctor Ledlie brought me in his bag;
he had a king-like beard, a long frock coat.
And so, when other children used to brag
of flying storks, or, loud in chorus, vote
for cabbages or goosegab bushes as
the magic places where they first appeared,
I always thought mine was a higher class,
a doctor's bag and stout King Edward's beard.

Those summer months she waited for the day
the doctor'd fetch me, my small mother sped
to a secluded seat upon the bank
beside the Lough somewhere near Helen's Bay,
to fill her mind with lovely thoughts, she said;
for such thoughts I perhaps have this to thank.

A HOLY PLACE

I loved to watch him shave, his splayed thumb pressed
on chin upraised, to let the stropped steel skim
the fluffed froth off. I felt I could not rest
till, one day, I should share this rite with him;
such skill, such peril, such unerring grace.
This was my daily vigil none might share;
that morning bathroom was a holy place,
one celebrant, one breathless worshipper.

This finished, he'd begin a lesser rite,
scrubbing my face, my neck, my hands, my knees,
wholly engaging me, in sheer delight
my stance entranced by some repeated spell
from Aesop, from Lamb's *Shakespeare*, Kingsley's *Greece*,
Gould's *Book of Moral Lessons*, William Tell.

MY SISTER

My only sister, Eileen, always was
protective sister for a timid boy;
half-roads to Mother, she could still enjoy
my easy games, was quick with the applause
she saw I needed. When our parents went
to concert or to meeting, made my tea.
When bigger, rougher boys grew violent,
hers was the ready arm defended me.

And with the years her uses multiplied,
taught me, for instance, how to tie my shoe,
and headed me by candlelight to bed,
and only once reported when I lied.
I should have liked a brother, it is true,
but that was in addition, not instead.

THE IRISH DIMENSION

With these folk gone, next door was tenanted
by a mild man, an Army Officer,
two girls, a boy, left in his quiet care,
his wife, their mother, being some years dead.
We shortly found that they were Catholics,
the very first I ever came to know.
To other friends they might be Teagues or Micks;
the lad I quickly found no sort of foe.

Just my own age. His Christian Brothers' School
to me seemed cruel. As an altar boy
he served with dread. His magazines were full
of faces, places, named, unknown to me.
Benburb, Wolfe Tone, Cuchullain, Fontenoy.
I still am grateful, Willie Morrissey.

CARNATIONS

They brought his coffin home and laid it on
the polished table in the dining room.
Though it was summer still, a mellow gloom
pervaded all, blinds down and curtains drawn.
Carnation wreaths – a little late that year –
lay round the open box when I stepped in;
I saw shirt-ruffles round the bearded chin;
the odour of those flowers was everywhere.

Once, long years after – I was seventy –
reading, companioned only by my thought,
a whiff of sweet carnations came to me.
It was that day the cleaning woman brought
a fistful in and thrust them in a vase –
I saw again that coffin, saw his face.

I LIE ALONE

I was promoted when Grandfather died,
taking his bed now in the top back room.
The mirrored wardrobe where he used to hide
his smuggled fruit still cidered its perfume.
I took all over, piled the mantel shelf
with books I owned, hung pictures on the wall
which I had been allowed to choose myself,
Murillo's *Shepherd* print, the crown of all.

I woke at dawn soon after, sensed he lay
beside me in the bed. I dared not stir,
but mused shut-eyed, how long I cannot say,
remembering he loved me in his way
as I loved him. No reason now for fear.
I reached my right hand out; no one was there.

THE GLENS

Groined by deep glens and walled along the west
by the bare hilltops and the tufted moors,
this rim of arable that ends in foam
has but to drop a leaf or snap a branch
and my hand twitches with the leaping verse
as hazel twig will wrench the straining wrists
for untapped jet that thrusts beneath the sod.

Not these my people, of a vainer faith
and a more violent lineage. My dead
lie in the steepled hillock of Kilmore
in a fat country rich with bloom and fruit.
My days, the busy days I owe the world,
are bound to paved unerring roads and rooms
heavy with talk of politics and art.
I cannot spare more than a common phrase
of crops and weather when I pace these lanes
and pause at hedge gap spying on their skill,
so many fences stretch between our minds.

I fear their creed as we have always feared
the lifted hand against unfettered thought.
I know their savage history of wrong
and would at moments lend an eager voice,
if voice avail, to set that tally straight.

And yet no other corner in this land
offers in shape and colour all I need
for sight to torch the mind with living light.

THE MAN FROM MALABAR

Here in this Irish room
the man from Malabar
sits cross-legged on the floor
and beats his little drum;
though no drum's here to beat,
his mimicry is such
that we imagine it
as true for sight as touch.

To that accompaniment
he lifts a wavering song,
meandering along,
on some heart's errand sent,
a winding jungle track,
a dancing village mode,
swaying and falling back
as the dark fingers bid.

And somewhere on the rim
of that strange haunting cry
a cadence makes its way,
an old song wanders home,
to summon to the thought
a country crossroads fair –
a strain some singer caught
out of the misty air.

THE COVENANTER'S GRAVE

One day they argued whence their family name
and quizzed their father. 'Ayrshire,' he replied.
'Three hundred years ago a preacher came
to plant us in the Antrim countryside;
his grave's at Donegore.' The elder son
wondered aloud if there'd still be a trace –
that name – his name – upon some lettered stone –
to show that he had found the proper place.

He travelled there, and in the churchyard sought
among the stones, aware that someone stared,
a woman from that house beyond the gate.
Her peremptory challenge proudly brought
the name for which he searched, deliberate.
'Youse were a long time comin',' she declared.

A HOUSE DEMOLISHED
spring 1981

They might have waited had they been aware
that I still lived, before they knocked it down.
Bricked-up and blind, our terrace still stood there
as in so many streets in this sick town.
Sealed off from sight, rooms hugged bright memories,
the kitchen with its range, the dining room,
its coal fire lit for small festivities,
the room upstairs where singing friends would come.
And in the top front bedroom I was born;
familiar with each vivid place I grew
to manhood; every window, stair and door
led to the widening scene my senses drew.
Walls, woodwork shattered, textures shredded, torn,
those haunted corners hoard my dreams no more.

THE CHRISTMAS RHYMERS, BALLYNURE, 1941
an old woman remembers

The Christmas Rhymers came again last year,
wee boys with blackened faces at the door,
not like those strapping lads that would appear,
dressed for the mummers' parts in times before,
to act the old play on the kitchen floor;
at warwork now or fighting overseas,
my neighbours' sons; there's hardly one of these
that will be coming back here any more.

I gave them coppers, bid them turn and go;
and as I watched that rueful regiment
head for the road, I felt that with them went
those songs we sang, the rhymes we used to know,
heartsore imagining the years without
The Doctor, Darkie, and Wee Divil Doubt.

FOR ROBERTA IN THE GARDEN

I know when you are at your happiest,
kneeling on mould, a trowel in your glove;
you raise your eyes and for a moment rest;
you turn a young-girl's face, like one in love.

Intent, entranced, this hour, in gardening,
surely to life's bright process you belong.
I wonder, when you pause, you do not sing,
for such a moment surely has its song.

THE HEDGEHOG: FOR R.

With shrewd snout the hedgehog
snuffles across the lawn
over the long shadows
of stilted hollyhock;
unpredicted presence,
its purposes unguessed,
threading a tiny life,
heart pulsing, hungry, warm,
slack spines dragging against
the prospering clover,
unresting, out of reach.

Its secret triggers set,
it seemed a symbol
for all timid strangeness,
all shy wildness, alert
to defend itself by
privacy, withdrawal;
a fellow creature lurked
within your heart and mine.

TO THE PEOPLE OF DRESDEN

Your famous city stood, plucked out of time,
a dream-pavilion set in porcelain,
where the masked dancers paced in stately mime
with grace no later age can now attain.
Then towards disaster all seemed swiftly drawn,
your cruel firestorm fuelling men's fears,
to shards all shattered, all those dancers gone,
in the dark Europe of my middle years.

But now that darkness breaks, and I have stood,
shouldered with thousands in your Altmarkt Square,
to swear my silent oath of brotherhood,
and join my lonely prayer to your vast prayer
that by the common will of common men
no war shall ever darken day again.

from FREEHOLD

from I Feathers on turf

We'd walked these roads before with quick delight
at tilt of roof-line or design of gate,
bright smears of light on Garron, or on the sea,
and how the wind's remembered by the tree,
naming the wild flowers, watching from the rocks
the diving cormorants, and the busy flocks
of dunlin landing where the bog-brown Dall
cuts through the seashore with a lazy scrawl,
and leaves a mounded tongue of sand whereon
the patriarchal heron stands alone.

And having gone back to the city's grey
autumnal gloom, the roaring crowded day,
the winter evenings with the curtained light,
and the mad engines thumping through the night,
we knew that from that gentle interval
rich moments had returned at words' recall,
spoken or read, or when the mind was caught
adrift and idle from the leash of thought.

I've long had witness certain images –
bare country phrases, old men's memories,
worn hafts of axes, cottage ornaments,
tea canisters, old bindings, potted plants,
cloud colours, whorls of shell or stranded weed,
feathers on turf or gaping husks of seed –

mixed with the figures that my meshy brain
must in its knots and tangled loops retain,
can, when the hand is ready, prompt again
the quiet verses that have strength to give
some lasting reason why I like to live.

But what seemed always underpinned by doubt
was that, when beating showers had flattened out
our footsteps from the mud, and when the land
wore no more track of us than tide-washed sand,
one shred should linger, hint or breath or touch,
above the roads and rocks beloved by each;
that fisherman with one more line to throw
or pausing farmer glancing up from plough
might even recall a word of all we said
or sometimes think he saw us on the road.

from II The lonely heart

In all his ways a just and kindly man
who set his steps as if to some grave plan
for purposes beyond all argument;
if there were voices he did not recount
their orders, but continued in his part,
that secret warrant safe against his heart;
wrought hard and unequivocally stood
for quality of life and brotherhood,
without defiance, in all charity
towards those who in themselves were not yet free.

He sang old songs, and in his crowded days
had lifted baton in his Master's praise,
later content to span his octaves, though
he'd now and then rejoice in cello-bow;

with watercolours never more than fair
repeated themes with undiminished care;
played moderate golf on summer Saturdays,
and wrote reviews when he'd the urge to praise,
served on committees if he liked the cause,
but neither won nor wanted long applause;
spoke when chance granted, without eloquence,
warmly sincere, with gentle common sense,
for all that gave life richness and should again
be the accepted right of workingmen,
as he judged all men who are worth their salt.
If error seemed to triumph, then the fault
lay not in evil, but in ignorance,
and would come right in time. He looked askance
at angry theories set to overthrow
the good-mixed error at a single blow,
and counselled patience: those who have recourse
to force would find their own rash end in force:
and so he wore through life unblemished name,
lonely at heart and innocent of fame.

This written, I have told you nothing of
the greatest man of all the men I love;
his little jokes, his gestures, his affection
that shrank surprised behind his circumspection,
his gentle patience and his silences,
his scribbled notes and numbered summaries
forgot in pocket; and his joy when you
suddenly found that all the time he knew
what you by tedious thought had sorted out;
his quiet sense of being clear of doubt,
yet not dogmatic in the peace achieved;
he had no need to tell what he believed:

the vast and varied knowledge in his head,
though seldom seemed there leisure enough to read;
he rather learnt by breathing than intent,
and freely taking just as freely spent.

. . . .

In my best moments feeling justly proud,
I wait his smile and slow approving nod,
but suddenly I know he is not here,
and have small faith that he is anywhere,
and I must chalk the little victories
for life and art and human decencies
as if on blackboard in a public place,
for chance of sleeve or weather to efface,
and never know them radically defined
in the bright lens of his translucent mind.

. . . .

Once in a seaside town with time to kill,
the windless winter-daylight ebbing chill,
the cafés shut till June, the shop blinds drawn,
only one pub yet open where a man
trundled his barrels off a dray with care,
and two men talking, small across the square,
I turned from broad street, down a red-brick row,
past prams in parlours and infrequent show
of thrusting bulbtips, till high steps and porch
and rigid statue signalised a church.
I climbed the granite past Saint Patrick's knees,
saw cross in stone, befingered, ringed with grease,

and water in a stoup with oily skin,
swung door on stall of booklets and went in
to the dim stained-glass cold interior
between low pews along a marble floor
to where the candles burned, still keeping pace
with ugly-coloured Stations of the Cross.
Two children tiptoed in and prayed awhile.
A shabby woman in a faded shawl
came hirpling past me then, and crumpled down,
crossing herself and mumbling monotone.

I stood and gazed across the altar rail
at the tall windows, cold and winter pale;
Christ and His Mother, Christ and Lazarus,
Christ watching Martha bustle round the house,
Christ crowned, with sceptre and a blessing hand.
I counted seven candles on the stand;
a box of matches of familiar brand
lay on a tray. It somehow seemed my right
to pay my penny and set up my light,
not to this coloured Christ nor to His Mother,
but single flame to sway with all the other
small earnest flames against the crowding gloom
which seemed that year descending on our time,
suppressed the fancy, smiled a cynic thought,
turned clicking heel on marble and went out.

Not this my fathers' faith: their walls are bare;
their comfort's all within, if anywhere.
I had gone there a vacant hour to pass,
to see the sculpture and admire the glass,
but left as I had come, a protestant,
and all unconscious of my yawning want;

too much intent on what to criticise
to give my heart the room to realise
that which endures the tides of time so long
cannot be always absolutely wrong;
not even with a friendly thought or human
for the two children and the praying woman.
The years since then have proved I should have stayed
and mercy might have touched me till I prayed.

For now I scorn no man's or child's belief
in any symbol that may succour grief
if we remember whence life first arose
and how within us yet that river flows;
and how the fabled shapes in dream's deep sea
still evidence our continuity
with being's seamless garment, web and thread.

O windblown grass upon the mounded dead,
O seed in crevice of the frost-split rock,
the power that fixed your root shall take us back,
though endlessly through aeons we are thrust
as luminous or unreflecting dust.

from III Townland of peace

Old John, my father's father, ran these roads
a hundred years ago with other lads
up the steep brae to school, or over the stile
to the far house for milk, or dragging the long mile
to see his mother buried. Every stride
with gable, gatepost, hedge on either side,
companioned so brought nearer my desire
to stretch my legs beside a poet's fire

in the next parish. As the road went by
with meadow and orchard, under a close sky,
and stook-lined field, and thatched and slated house,
and apples heavy on the crouching boughs,
I moved beside him. Change was strange and far
where a daft world gone shabby choked with war
among the crumpled streets or in the plains
spiked with black fire-crisped rafters and buckled lines,
from Warsaw to the Yangtze, where the slow-
phrased people learn such thought that scourge and blow
may school them into strength to find the skill
for new societies of earth and steel,
but here's the age they've lost.
                              The boys I met
munching their windfalls, drifting homeward late,
are like that boy a hundred years ago,
the same bare kibes, the heirloom rags they show;
but they must take another road in time.
Across the sea his fortune summoned him
to the brave heyday of the roaring mills
where progress beckoned with a million wheels

. . . .

Now and for ever through the change-rocked years,
I know my corner in the universe;
my corner, this small region limited
in space by sea, in the time by my own dead,
who are its compost, by each roving sense
henceforward mobilised in its defence,
against the sickness that has struck mankind,
mass-measured, mass-infected, mass-resigned.

Against the anthill and the beehive state
I hold the right of man to stay out late,
to sulk and laugh, to criticise or pray,
when he is moved, at any hour of day,
to vote by show of hands or sit at home,
or stroll on Sunday with a vasculum,
to sing or act or play or paint or write
in any mode that offers him delight.

I hold my claim against the mammoth powers
to crooked roads and accidental flowers,
to corn with poppies fabulously red,
to trout in rivers, and to wheat in bread,
to food unpoisoned, unpolluted air,
and easy pensioned age without a care
other than time's mortality must bring
to any shepherd, commissar, or king.

But these small rights require a smaller stage
than the vast forum of the nations' rage,
for they imply a well-compacted space
where every voice declares its native place,
townland, townquarter, county at the most,
the local word not ignorantly lost
in the smooth jargon, bland and half alive,
which wears no clinging burr upon its sleeve
to tell the ground it grew from, and to prove
there is for sure a plot of earth we love.

from IV The glittering sod

Mine is historic Ulster, battlefield
of Gael and Planter, certified and sealed
by blood, and what is stronger than the blood,
by images and folkways understood
but dimly by the wits, yet valid still
in word and gesture, name of house or hill,
and by the shapes of men whose texture was
determined by the nature of the place,
flogged by the strong wind, soothed by the soft rain,
flushed by the April sunshine's gay champagne,
shod by the heather, heeled by the yielding moss,
till, wayward and persistent as the grass,
they kept their roots, or when chance drove them off,
held earth about them close and strong enough
to feed their stature with new skies to fill,
from Alexander Irvine back to Colmcille.

And we remaining here are what we are,
not by conjunction of this moon or star
scored on a tablet, drawn in desert sand,
but by the tilt and angle of this land,
last edge of Europe, cliff against the west
stemming the strong tides with its broken coast,
wedged in cleft-stick of sudden cloud and sun,
rimmed like a metal cup to measure the rain,
sodden and loaded with time's dripping weight,
chilled by the slow declension of the light,
when the great scab of ice withdrawing tore
the long glens sloping to the eastern shore,
for, after that, sick from the swamping wave,
the tall men scrambled, glad to be alive,

from their small vessels grounded in the reeds,
to light their fires and build their wicker sheds
on the safe flint-rich hills above the beast-
thronged forest and the bitter marsh waste;
first landed of those driven refugee
by Europe's pulse thrust westward endlessly,
to yield a living space for men who came
with metal point and horse and lintelled tomb
from the wide Asian plains.

. . . .

I urge but this. When you have stood awhile
and watched the shadows running mile on mile
over the heather and the wind-bleached grass
where heroes strode, where heroes still may pass;
when you have flung your pebbles in the sea
from the black cliff; when, stepping leisurely,
you've come upon a grey-walled meeting house
where lichened headstones tilt in dumb carouse,
and know your people lie there, clay in clay;
when you have heard the loud drum far away
throb through the stillness of a summer night,
you too have this illimitable right.

Just so with me. Against this weight of pride
for years I'd set my wits, instead I'd tried
to wring a simple meaning out of sense,
equipping my slow mind for swift response
to painted panel or to printed book;
yet every road I travelled brought me back,
back to the sunlight on the glittering sod,
back to my fathers and their silent God.

ULSTER NAMES

I take my stand by the Ulster names,
each clean hard name like a weathered stone;
Tyrella, Rostrevor, are flickering flames:
the names I mean are the Moy, Malone,
Strabane, Slieve Gullion and Portglenone.

Even suppose that each name were freed
from legend's ivy and history's moss,
there'd be music still in, say, Carrick-a-rede,
though men forget it's the rock across
the track of the salmon from Islay and Ross.

The names of a land show the heart of the race;
they move on the tongue like the lilt of a song.
You say the name and I see the place –
Drumbo, Dungannon, Annalong.
Barony, townland, we cannot go wrong.

You say Armagh, and I see the hill
with the two tall spires or the square low tower;
the faith of Patrick is with us still;
his blessing falls in a moonlit hour,
when the apple orchards are all in flower.

You whisper Derry. Beyond the walls
and the crashing boom and the coiling smoke,
I follow that freedom which beckons and calls
to Colmcille, tall in his grove of oak,
raising his voice for the rhyming folk.

County by county you number them over;
Tyrone, Fermanagh ... I stand by a lake,
and the bubbling curlew, the whistling plover
call over the whins in the chill daybreak
as the hills and the waters the first light take.

Let Down be famous for care-tilled earth,
for the little green hills and the harsh grey peaks,
the rocky bed of the Lagan's birth,
the white farm fat in the August weeks.
There's one more county my pride still seeks.

You give it the name and my quick thoughts run
through the narrow towns with their wheels of trade,
to Glenballyemon, Glenaan, Glendun,
from Trostan down to the braes of Layde,
for there is the place where the pact was made.

But you have as good a right as I
to praise the place where your face is known,
for over us all is the selfsame sky;
the limestone's locked in the strength of the bone,
and who shall mock at the steadfast stone?

So it's Ballinamallard, it's Crossmaglen,
it's Aughnacloy, it's Donaghadee,
it's Magherafelt breeds the best of men,
I'll not deny it. But look for me
on the moss between Orra and Slievenanee.

Postscript, 1984

Those verses surfaced thirty years ago
when time seemed edging to a better time,
most public voices tamed, those loud untamed
as seasonal as tawdry pantomime,
and over my companionable land
placenames still lilted like a childhood rime.

The years deceived; our unforgiving hearts,
by myth and old antipathies betrayed,
flared into sudden acts of violence
in daily shocking bulletins relayed,
and through our dark dream-clotted consciousness
hosted like banners in some black parade.

Now with compulsive resonance they toll:
Banbridge, Ballykelly, Darkley, Crossmaglen,
summoning pity, anger and despair,
by grief of kin, by hate of murderous men
till the whole tarnished map is stained and torn,
not to be read as pastoral again.

INDEX OF TITLES

A Birthday Rhyme for Roberta 95
A Father's Death 104
A Happy Boy 106
A Holy Place 112
A House Demolished 120
A Local Poet 99
A Mobile Mollusc 98
An Irishman in Coventry 53
An Ulsterman 68
April Awake 58

Balloons and Wooden Guns 107
Because I Paced My Thought 23
Black and White 74

Carnations 115
Chinese Fluteplayer 77
Colour 27
from Conacre 1
Cultra Manor: The Ulster Folk Museum 91

East Antrim Winter 10
Emily Dickinson 78
Encounter Nineteen Twenty 97
Et Tu in Arcadia Vixisti 87

First Corncrake 9
First Snow in the Glens 26
Footing Turf 59

For a Moment of Darkness Over the Nations 100
For Roberta in the Garden 122
from Freehold 125
From the Chinese of Wang Li Shi 76
From the Tibetan 85
Frost 16

Ghosts 17
Gloss, on the Difficulties of Translation 67
Grey and White 80

Hedgehog 43

I Lie Alone 116
I Write For ... 82

Jacob and the Angel 52

Landscape 28
Leaf 14
Load 15
Lyric 12
Lyric 13

Man Fish and Bird 32
Mary Hagan, Islandmagee, 1919 89
May Altar 62
My Grandmother's Garter 56
My Sister 113

Mycenae and Epidaurus 20
Mykonos 19

Neither an Elegy nor a
 Manifesto 92

O Country People 30
Once Alien Here 8
Orchard Country 110
Ossian's Grave, Lubitavish,
 County Antrim 49

Rite, Lubitavish, Glenaan 44

Scissors for a One-Armed Tailor 79
Skypiece 81
from Sonnets for Roberta (1954) 105
Street Names 70
Substance and Shadow 96
Sunset over Glenaan 60

The Ballad 63
The Bell 65
The Blossomed Thorn 103
The Christmas Rhymers,
 Ballynure, 1941 121
The Coasters 71
The Colony 36
The Covenanter's Grave 119

The Dilemma 69
The Doctor's Bag 111
The Frontier 51
The Glens 117
The Glens of Antrim 102
The Green Shoot 24
The Hedgehog: For R. 123
The Hill-Farm 66
The Irish Dimension 114
The King's Horses 90
The Magician 109
The Man from Malabar 118
The Municipal Gallery
 Revisited, October 1954 47
The Owl 45
The Ram's Horn 29
The Romantic 101
The Scar 88
The Search 83
The Stoat 41
The Storm 75
The Swathe Uncut 11
The Volunteer 108
The Wake 64
The Watchers 42
To the People of Dresden 124
Turf-Carrier on Aranmore 21

Ulster Names 135

Whit Monday 55